Tiffany's Addiction:

Director's cut

I0547368

D M Gaines

Tiffany's Addiction: Director's cut

Editing and cover design by
Earvin Taze Watters Jr.
ezatcreations@yahoo.com
Revised August 2015

www.newflavorbooksandpublishingllc.com
New Flavor Books is an imprint of New Flavor Books & Publishing
LLC

New Flavor Books & Publishing LLC
P.O. Box 603323 Cleveland, Ohio 44103

Dedication

This book is dedicated to all women that may have a sexual dysfunction that may be due to a past sexual abuse. Don't be afraid to seek help and find answers.

Acknowledgement

I would like to thank my daughter Brittiny Roseberry, without you none of this would have been possible, I love you dearly. I would like to thank my editor Earvin Taze Watters Jr. only the Lord knows how this book would have turned out without you, Thank you, brother. To my mother Carol Marie Gaines, thanks for having me. Thanks to my brother Twone for having my back. Thanks to Poetic Gangster for the inspiration and guidance. Also thanks to Fred Robertson my best critic, what's up dawg we got it done. Lastly, thanks to everyone that believed in me and made me see that I have something to give.

Chapter 1

"That's it right there!" Tiffany begged Greg as he pounded her. He had her legs over his shoulders as he fucked her. To him, Tiffany had some of the best pussy that he ever had.

He knew that he was wrong for fucking his cousin's wife. But after turning down so many of her advances he had given in and has been hooked ever since.

Tiffany was wild and there wasn't a limit to the things she would do sexually. He pulled out of her pussy and pulled her up putting his dick in her mouth. She greedily engulfed him, sucking intensively and making slurping sounds. Greg knew that he couldn't hold back any longer. He gripped the back of the couch and braced himself. His legs began to shake as he busted off in her mouth. Tiffany hungrily swallowed his cum.

"Damn girl you are a beast!" Greg told her as he got up and started getting dressed.

Tiffany laid there thinking, "Girl, you are crazy fucking your husband's cousin in your own house. Someone could pop up at any time."

Tiffany tried to focus but her mind drifted off. She could see visions of herself at the young age of eleven having sex with numerous boys in the projects. She just couldn't pinpoint when it was that she had become so obsessed with sex. If she could figure that out, then she could possibly save her marriage to Cliff.

Tiffany and Cliff had been married for two years. Before they were married she was cheating on Cliff, even with his best friend Mike on the day of their wedding. Greg told her bye as he was leaving out the door, but Tiffany was in another world. She laid there thinking about her wedding day.

β

She was downstairs in a room under the chapel getting ready, when she heard a tap at the door. She wasn't fully dressed and was hesitant about opening the door. She cracked it and there stood Mike, her soon to be husband's best friend. He pushed the door opened and she backed up "What are you doing?"

"I have to get my last piece of this pussy before you get married."

"Are you crazy? Everybody is here."

"If you'd stop prolonging, we could be through." he told her as he led her over to the table. He bent her over the table, lifted up her slip and pulled her panties down. He pulled his dick out of his pants and slid up in her. Tiffany let out a sigh. She could not believe that it was her wedding day and she was being fucked by her fiancé's best friend, who was also the best man. To top it off, it was feeling so good. It excited her to be getting fucked while everyone was upstairs preparing for the wedding.

β

A door slammed closed, snapping Tiffany back to the present. She quickly jumped up and slipped her pants on. "Hey ma," Angie said as she entered the living room.

"Why are you home so early?"

"They had a fire drill, and let us go early."

Angie is Tiffany's 14-year old daughter. "Well, make sure that you do your homework and clean up your room." Tiffany told Angie as she headed up stairs.

Tiffany had three other kids, besides Angie. She knew that she was lucky. Cliff married her even though she had four kids by four different men. He treated each of her kids as if they were his own and Tiffany loved him for that. She knew that she needed to get some help if she wanted to keep their marriage together.

Tiffany grabbed the phone book off of the nightstand, sat on the bed and turned to the "P" section. She started looking up psychiatrists. She scrolled until she came upon a Dr. Sullivan. She grabbed a pen off of the stand and circled the number. She picked up the phone and dialed the number, someone answered on the second ring, "Hello,

Dr. Sullivan's office. How may I help you?"

Tiffany hesitated for a minute, not knowing if she should go through with it or not. "Yes," she got up the courage, "My name is Tiffany Smith and I would like to make an appointment to see Dr. Sullivan." she said nervously.

"Are you a regular patient?"

"No, this will be my first time seeing her."

"I can fit you in for this Thursday at nine o'clock, will that be okay?"

"Yes, that will be fine."

"Okay, see you then." Tiffany hung up the phone and sat there for a minute. She was trying to think of an excuse that she could give Cliff as to why she was going to see a psychiatrist.

"Maybe I can just hide it from him." she thought to herself.

She went into the bathroom and cleaned up, so that she could prepare dinner. She knew that Cliff and the other kids would be home in a short while.

Chapter 2

Tiffany was in the kitchen, preparing dinner when Angie walked in.

"Ma, do you need me to help you with anything?" "You can set the table for me and make some Kool-Aid."

"Okay," Angie responded.

Tiffany made fried fish, macaroni, and cornbread. Just when she was getting finished Keisha and Donte came through the door.

"Where is Kiki?" Tiffany asked them.

"He dropped us off and said that he would be back." Donte told her.

"That boy loves running those streets. You guys go and wash your hands, then come sit down to eat." Tiffany made a plate for Cliff and put it up. Cliff was a hustler and there was never a set time that he would come in. She fixed herself a plate, then sat down in the living room and ate. After eating she dozed off.

Cliff shook her awake about eleven o'clock, "Damn girl, you do have a bed you know?"

"I was waiting on you so that I could warm your food up."

"The only thing that I'm hungry for is you. Let's go upstairs and get naked." Tiffany smiled, she jumped up and headed upstairs. She was glad that she had showered earlier and got Greg's scent off of her. She entered the bedroom with Cliff right on her heels. They both

stripped down naked and climbed in the bed. Cliff started off sucking on her titties, and then trailed his tongue down to her pussy. He used his hands to separate her pussy lips and began sucking her pussy. Tiffany groaned in pleasure as she put both of her hands on his head. She closed her eyes, but quickly opened them back up when a vision of her ex-lover Merv, popped up in her head. She got up, pushed Cliff down then straddled him. She lowered herself onto him, putting both of her hands on his chest. After only going up and down on him twice, Cliff was ready to cum. Tiffany seen his face start to contort and tried to slow down.

Their biggest problem was that Cliff was a premature ejaculator. Most of the time he would finish before Tiffany got off. This night was no different. Less than five minutes into the act Cliff had cum, rolled over and fell asleep.

Tiffany laid there feeling unsatisfied. She felt the urge to smoke. She got up and put on some clothes, so that she could walk to the corner store. What she put on really wasn't fit for her to leave the house in. She put on some cut off jean shorts that left the bottom of her ass cheeks hanging out and a tank top with no bra underneath.

As she walked to the store, the cool night air made her nipples hard. She made her way the few blocks to the Arab store. When she stepped in, Hasan was behind the counter. Hasan is the son of the owner of the store. He was twenty three years old and got along with all the blacks in the neighborhood. He would try to hit on all the pretty black girls that came into the store.

Hasan had been yearning for some black pussy all day. Being a Muslim he had never experienced untamed sex until he had it with a black woman. He had tried to hit on Tiffany many times. She would flirt back but never gave him any real play. He figured that tonight he would try again.

"Hey Tiffany, what are you doing out this late at night all by yourself?"

"I need to get me a pack of Kools."

"One pack of Kools coming up," he reached up and grabbed a pack of king sized Kools off of the shelf and handed them to her.

Tiffany went to pay him the money and he pushed it back to her.

"Tiffany, do you know about computers?"

"Yeah why?"

"We just got a new computer and I cannot get it to come on. Do you think that you can take a look at it for me?"

"I can do that for you." Hasan came from behind the counter, locked the door and put up the closed sign. He then led Tiffany into the back. She was surprised that the office had a bar, a couch and a flat screen TV.

Hasan showed her to the computer. Tiffany pulled out the chair and sat in front of the computer, it was an Apple computer. She tried to turn it on, but the screen stayed blank. She asked Hasan did he have the instructions. He got them and handed them to her. After reading them, she noticed that some of the wires were crossed. She corrected them and the computer booted up. Tiffany stood up.

"Thank you, let me give you a drink."

"Okay,"

He made her a shot of Grey Goose.

"So Tiffany, why you do not give Hasan any play?"

"You know me like you and can do things for you." "Hasan I am married."

"Me know that you are married. In my country, us men can have many wives. Women are meant to share. You are too beautiful to belong to one man." Hasan said.

He approached her and put his hand on her face. Tiffany felt a tingle go through her body and her pussy got wet.

"Hasan I love my husband."

"Do not worry he will not know. This is not about love, it is about pleasure. Please let me give it to you." he said as he kissed her. He put his hands around her and she melted into him. He led her over to the couch and began undressing her. Once he had her naked, he admired her rich, chocolate colored body.

"Tiffany, you have a beautiful body. Your pussy is very pretty also. Please bend over and spread your legs, I must taste you."

Tiffany bent over the couch and spread her legs. Hasan knelt down behind her and started sucking her pussy from the back.

Tiffany could not believe how good he was eating her pussy. He caused her whole body to tingle. She wanted his tongue further up in her, so she reached back took both of her hands and spread her ass cheeks. Hasan was so far up in her pussy, that it seemed as if her ass cheeks were on the sides of his face.

All of a sudden he stopped, got up and started taking off his pants. Tiffany stayed in the same position, but turned her head around to see what he was doing. She wanted to see what he was working with. When he dropped his boxers, she was surprised that he was holding. His dick scared her. It was about nine inches, but it was uncircumcised and had a curve in it. She reached back and felt it. Feeling it pulsate in her hand. She then guided it to her pussy.

Hasan sunk all the way in to the hilt. He started fucking her slowly. She did not know if it was the curve in his dick or him being uncircumcised, but she was experiencing a feeling that she had never felt before in her life. Her whole body shook uncontrollably. She blurted out, "Damn! Hasan, your dick is good!" Hasan started fucking in frenzy. He started talking in Arabic. He gripped Tiffany by the hips and pounded her until he busted a nut.

They both collapsed on the couch next to each other. Tiffany felt like going to sleep right there, but she knew that she had to get home.

Reluctantly, she got dressed. Hasan followed her lead. Once they were dressed, they headed back out front. Hasan asked, "Was me good, no?"

Tiffany smiled, "You were very good." she hurried and left out of the store, knowing that if she stayed any longer that they would end up fucking again. She turned back around and handed Hasan back the pack of cigarettes. He stood there looking at her confused.

"I don't need them anymore." she told him. Hasan stuck his chest out and beamed with pride as he watched her walk away.

Tiffany got in at two in the morning. Everyone was asleep. She went into the bathroom, washed up, came out and climbed back in the bed with Cliff.

D M Gaines

Chapter 3

Angie lay awake in her bed. She heard her mother come in and wondered where she had been. She knew that her mother was cheating on Cliff. One day, she had come home from school early and seen her mother getting fucked by Cliff's best friend Mike. They did not notice her and she quickly left back out of the house.

That wasn't the first time that she had witnessed her mother having sex. She remembered when she was younger. She woke up in the middle of the night to use the bathroom. When she went to pass her mother's room the door was cracked and she heard noises. She peeked in her mother's room and there were two men in there with her. One was having sex with her from behind while the other one had his penis in her mouth.

She had confused feelings about her mother. She figured that it was because of her mother's sexual behavior, that she did not know who her father was. She often resented her mother for that.

Angie had started having sex over a year ago, at the age of thirteen and couldn't understand why her mother liked it so much. She had yet to experience any pleasure from sex. She only did it to please whoever she was with.

β

Tiffany slept late. She did not wake up until 11:30 in the morning. Cliff was already gone. She laid there in bed thinking about the night before. That was her first time being with a foreigner and he had fucked her better than any black man ever had. She thought that if Cliff could fuck her like that, then maybe he could satisfy her.

The telephone rang, "Hello?"

"Girl, what's up?" asked her friend Tiny.

"Nothing, just getting up."

"If you are just getting up, that means you had some good dick last night. Cliff finally stepped his game up huh?"

"Girl please,"

"Bitch! Where did you get it from then?"

"Hasan down at the 24-hour mini mart."

"You fucked one of those camel riding mother fuckers?"

"Bitch! Don't sleep, that camel riding mother fucker fucked me like I have never been fucked before. Plus his dick is as long as a camel's leg."

"Hoe, stop lying."

"I'm serious! That foreign mother fucker got a ten inch, uncircumcised dick with a curve in it and he knows how to work it."

"Shit, you might got to introduce me to his ass. We can have us a three-way like the old days."

"Girl you know that I'm married now."

"Bitch! Who do you think you're talking to? Your more of a hoe now than you was before you married Cliff. Why did you marry him anyway knowing that one nigga, or at least he can't satisfy you?"

"Because I was ready to settle down. I really love Cliff. I think something is wrong with me. I have made an appointment to see a psychiatrist to get some help."

"Hoe you ain't crazy, you're just a freak."

"There has got to be a reason for my behavior. All I think about is sex all the time, and now I am thinking of other people, when I am with Cliff."

"So your ass is going to a shrink."

"Yeah,"

"Does Cliff know?"

"I haven't decided if I am going to tell him or not. He doesn't know that I have a problem."

"Well, girl, I hope shit works out for you. If you need me, just call."

"Thanks Tiny, you know I love you right?"

"Yeah, I love you too girl, bye." Tiffany appreciated Tiny's call.

They had been friends for over ten years. They were real close, having been intimate with each other as well as participating in many threesomes together. They knew each other's secrets. So, Tiffany felt at ease telling her about Hasan and going to see a psych. She knew that she could turn to Tiny for support.

Chapter 4

The house was empty. The kids were at school and Cliff was out in the streets.

Tiffany went to the kitchen and made herself some breakfast. She sat at the kitchen table and ate her eggs and toast. While sitting there, flashes of the night before entered her mind again. She could still see and feel Hasan inside of her. Her pussy started to heat up. She said to herself, "Oh Lord!"

She jumped up and went upstairs. She entered her bedroom and went over to her dresser. She pulled out the bottom drawer and pulled out a DVD and a big, black, shiny vibrator, that she had named Mr. Bender. She put in the DVD, which was a porno called, "Butt Man 2"

She slid out of her clothes, and then sat on the end of her bed. She inserted Mr. Bender, and let out a sigh of relief. It gave her a calming effect. She stroked herself with the vibrator as she watched a tall, dark, black guy with a ten inch penis fuck a Spanish chick in her ass. He was fucking the girl in an animalistic way with a lot of force. Also he was making animal like sounds.

Tiffany looked at the girl's face, which held a look of pure bliss. Tiffany closed her eyes and envisioned that she was the girl in the movie. She started fucking herself with the vibrator at a fast pace. She started talking in the form of two persons.

"Shit, that's it right there, fuck this pussy. Damn this pussy is good, it's so wet."

"I'm about to cum! I'm about to cum!" her body shook and convulsed. She had a big climax, and fell back on the bed to catch her breath. Once she caught her breath, she stood up and walked over to the mirror. She stood there naked looking at herself, "Girl, what is wrong with you? You have to get yourself together."

Tiffany was thirty two years old, with her oldest child being seventeen and the youngest being twelve. She still had a nice body. Her thighs were firm and her breast still sat up high. Her ass was still round as a basketball. As far as looks, that was a different story.

Though she wasn't ugly, she wasn't pretty either, and her face looked like it could use a year worth of ProActiv. She stood there wondering if how she felt about herself played a part in how she became addicted to sex. She shook that thought because she felt what was wrong with her could be physical.

One of her ex-boyfriends, used to always tell her that she had a white liver, because she always craved sex, as much as three or four times a day sometimes.

Her appointment was for the next day at nine, and she was hoping that Dr. Sullivan would be able to give her answers.

She went into the bathroom, cleaned herself up, went back into the room and put the vibrator and DVD back in its hiding place. She then went downstairs to clean up.

Chapter 5

Kiki had cut out of school and was sitting over at Sharon's house. Sharon was one of the many girls that Kiki was fucking. He found it hard to be with or to trust one girl. His relationship with his mother had scarred him. She had him when she was fifteen, and by the time he was five he could understand what was going on around him. He started to take in his mother's behavior with all the different men that she would mess with.

What truly traumatized him was up until he was ten years old she had him thinking that Keith was his father. After taking a paternity test for child support, it was revealed that Keith wasn't his father.

Tiffany gave the agency two more men's name. The agency tracked the men down and tested them. Both men came back negative. After that Tiffany gave up searching, leaving Kiki with a void feeling of not having a father and resentment towards her for fucking with so many men in the same time frame.

Based on how he viewed his mother, he thought all women were hoes and he treated them as such.

Sharon came out of her room wearing nothing but a t-shirt. She stood in front of him, and put her hands on her hips. Kiki looked up and seen the look of anger on her face.

"What are you tripping about?"

"Why do you keep doing this to me?"

"What are you talking about?"

"Are you going to fuck all of my friends? I just got off the phone with Renee, and she said that you fucked her and that she might be pregnant by you."

"So what! Look Sharon we are only fucking, so don't take it for no more than what it's worth."

"I understand that, but why my friends?"

"I'm not fucking them because they are your friends. I fuck them because I am attracted to them, it has nothing to do with you."

"I think this is going to be our last time doing anything. I can't keep doing this. I really like you and you keep making me look like a fool." Sharon said.

"I hear all that, and it's your choice, but you know that you are going to miss this." he told her as he unzipped his pants and pulled out his dick. Sharon couldn't believe his cockiness. He was so arrogant and disrespectful. The killing part is that she was addicted to him.

"Come here and let daddy dick feed you." As if in a trance she walked over to him, knelt between his legs and lowered her mouth onto him. Kiki spread his arms out on the couch and put his head back as he enjoyed the feeling.

He knew that he was wrong for the way that he treated Sharon, but he felt that no woman was worth being respected. After Sharon finished giving him head he got up and left without as much as saying goodbye.

Chapter 6

Tiffany was in the kitchen cooking when Angie, Donte and Keisha walked in.

"Hey ma," said Angie.

"Hey baby, are y'all hungry?" They all shook their heads in agreement that they were.

"Go upstairs and get yourselves together, then come back down to the table." They all marched upstairs. Tiffany started fixing their plates. She wondered about Donte, who always seemed withdrawn. He never spoke unless you spoke to him first. She figured that she would have to have a talk with him someday.

She became startled, when she felt a hand on her ass. She quickly turned around and there stood Cliff. She was surprised at the fact that he had come home so early. He pulled her to him and kissed her passionately in the mouth.

Tiffany's body reacted instantly, and she started heating up. Cliff put his hand under her dress. She did not have on any panties, and he slid two of his fingers into her pussy. Tiffany closed her eyes and moaned. She forgot all about the kids being on their way down to eat.

She heard a sound as if someone was clearing their throat and looked up. The kids were all standing there. Tiffany quickly tried to straighten herself up, while Cliff removed his fingers from her pussy, and gave the kids a look as if they had caught him with his hands in the cookie jar. The kids just giggled and took a seat. Tiffany fixed herself a plate and sat down.

Everybody was there except Kiki. It was a real family setting. Tiffany did not want to spoil the mood by dropping the bomb that she was going to see a psychiatrist, so she kept quiet. Cliff spoke, "So, how was everybody's day?" The girls said okay, but Donte remained silent.

"What's up with you Donte?" Cliff asked.

"Nothing,"

"Why are you always so quiet?"

Donte hunched his shoulders, "I don't know."

Cliff thought that Donte was too timid, even feminine maybe. He decided that he would start spending more time with him, to try to toughen him up. He felt obligated to do so, being as his real father wasn't around.

"Me and you are going to hang out this weekend, okay champ?" "Alright," Donte said timidly.

They finished dinner and Tiffany told the kids to do the dishes. She and Cliff went upstairs to their bedroom to finish what they had started earlier. Soon as they entered the room, Cliff stripped out of his clothes, threw her on the bed and entered her. Within five minutes he was through. He rolled over, curled up in a fetal position and went to sleep.

Tiffany laid there staring at the ceiling. She thought about going to see Hasan, but wanted to control her will. She tried to force herself to go to sleep.

She eventually dozed off for about an hour. She woke up yearning for a cigarette. She got up out of bed and quietly slipped back into her dress. Without putting on any panties, she headed out of the door. She headed down to the mini mart.

When she stepped into the store, she was disappointed that Hasan was not behind the counter. It was his brother Abdullah. She stepped up to the counter and asked for a pack of king sized Kools. While he was ringing them up, Hasan walked out of the back.

"Tiffany, you are back so soon." Tiffany smiled.

Abdullah spoke, "So, this is the girl that you talk about?"

"Yes, yes brother. She is a gift from Allah to man."

Tiffany stood there looking confused. Hasan rushed over to the door and locked it.

"Tiffany, my brother has yet to experience the American woman. You must show him, what you showed me last night." Tiffany stood there dumbfounded, but started thinking that maybe she should go out with a bang, seeing as she planned on becoming a new person the next day.

Hasan grabbed her by the hand and led her into the back, with Abdullah following behind them.

"Please, undress for us." Hasan told Tiffany. She lifted her dress up over her head and stood before them naked.

"See brother, no underwear, American women are very different, you agree? No?" Abdullah looked at Tiffany as if he wanted to eat her.

"Yes, yes, very different." Hasan approached Tiffany. He reached out and grabbed one of her tits. He bent his head and put her tittie into his mouth. He stopped and turned to his brother.

"Come, come, enjoy."

Abdullah quickly walked over to Tiffany and followed his brother's lead. He put Tiffany's other tittie into his mouth and started sucking on it. Tiffany took her hands and ran them through both of their hair. Her titties were one of her hot zones and the two brothers had her on fire. She felt herself cumming from just having her titties sucked, or she thought that maybe it was just the fact that she was being freaked by two foreigners, that had her so excited.

Hasan stopped sucking her tittie.

"We must fuck you now my queen." Hasan started taking his clothes off, with his brother following his lead. Hasan then led Tiffany over to the couch, where he began removing the pillows. To Tiffany's surprise the couch turned into a let out bed. Hasan folded it out.

"Tiffany you get on your hands and knees. We do it doggy style, as you say."

Tiffany got on the bed in the doggy style position. Hasan climbed on the bed behind her got on his knees and entered her. Abdullah was still standing in the middle of the floor not knowing what to do.

Hasan looked over at him, "Brother come, she give you head, get in the front."

Abdullah nervously walked over to the bed, with his dick sticking straight up in the air. Once he was in front of Tiffany, she reached out and grabbed his dick. The feel of her hand on his dick made his body shiver. She took him into her mouth, while using her hands to cuff his balls.

Abdullah's eyes rolled into the back of his head. He had never experienced such a feeling before. It was actually his first time getting a blow job. That was a sexual act that was not practiced in his country.

Hasan picked up his pace, while saying, "Your pussy is so good, Tiffany. You are very wet." His talking excited Tiffany more and she began bucking back on his dick. Abdullah saw how well his brother was getting it.

"Brother, we switch?"

"Okay, okay." Hasan slid out of Tiffany and he and Abdullah switched positions.

Tiffany started sucking Hasan's dick, while Abdullah banged her from behind.

Abdullah did not have as much control as his brother, and Tiffany's pussy was too good for him to handle. In less than two minutes of being inside of her, Abdullah's face started to contort. He grunted as he emptied himself inside of her. Hasan seen his brother's body spasm, and knew what was going on.

He laughed, "It is too good for you, brother?" Abdullah looked embarrassed.

"Sorry," he said as he got up from the bed.

"There is nothing to be sorry about. Her pussy is like magic." Hasan told him. "Tiffany me get ball deep in you, no?" Hasan stated as he pulled his dick out of her mouth. He had her lay down on her back, with her head being at the edge of the bed. He called Abdullah over, "You hold her legs for me." He took both of Tiffany's legs, put them together and pushed them straight back over her head, leaving her pussy sticking out like a flower blooming up out of the ground.

Abdullah grabbed her ankles and pushed her legs down until her knees were almost touching her forehead. Laterally, Hasan entered Tiffany, and sunk in ball deep. To Tiffany it felt like he was in her stomach. Hasan pulled out and Tiffany's pussy made a popping sound. He put his dick back in and slowly started long dicking Tiffany. Tiffany shook her head back and forth. She was in ecstasy and came within seconds. Her cum coated Hasan's dick and her pussy clung to him, as if it belonged there. Hasan sped his rhythm up and started slamming into her with force. Abdullah just looked on in amazement, as his brother fucked the hell out of Tiffany.

"Do her, brother, she is an animal." Abdullah's urging only made Hasan go faster. Tiffany reached out with both of her arms and gripped the sheets as she came again. Hasan felt his self about to cum.

"Here it comes, Tiffany!" he said as he sunk all the way into her. He nutted in her so powerfully, that Tiffany thought that she could taste his cum in her throat.

After Hasan got up, Tiffany laid there for about five minutes trying to get her senses back. Then they all got dressed and headed back out front. All the while, Abdullah felt the need to keep apologizing.

"I do better next time." Tiffany just smiled as she left.

Tiffany walked back to the house and crept upstairs to the bedroom. When she entered her room, she was surprised to see that Cliff was not in the bed. Her heart instantly started to race. She heard a toilet flush and the bathroom door open. Cliff walked in, with a twisted look on his face.

"Where the hell have you been?"

"I went to get me a pack of cigarettes from the store."

"That's bullshit! I've been sitting up over an hour wondering where the hell you were at. The store is only five minutes away. So where the hell were you?"

"I did not want to tell you, but I have a doctor's appointment at nine o'clock in the morning. I have been feeling sick for a while, and I have decided to see a doctor to find out what is wrong with me. I could not sleep from being so nervous, so I went to the store, got a pack of cigarettes and just took a walk."

"Why haven't you been told me that you were sick?"

"I wanted to find out what was exactly wrong with me, before I told you."

"Do you need me to go with you?"

"No, I will be alright, I'm probably just over reacting."

Cliff climbed back into bed, and Tiffany let out a sigh of relief. She knew that was a close call. She undressed and climbed into bed.

She snuggled up to Cliff and fell asleep.

Chapter 7

At eight O'clock the next morning Tiffany headed out the door on her way to her doctor's visit. She walked down to the bus stop. Within five minutes she was on the bus and on her way downtown.

She arrived at the doctor's office at 8:50am. She walked up to the receptionist.

"Excuse me. My name is Tiffany Smith and I have a nine O'clock appointment with Dr. Sullivan."

"Okay, please have a seat and I will let her know that you are here."

"Thank you" Tiffany said as she turned to go take a seat in the waiting area.

There were two other people sitting in there. Tiffany wondered what they were there for. One of them was a man, and Tiffany could not help but stare at him. He was very attractive to her. Her pussy started to get wet just from looking at him.

She broke her stare, and reached over and grabbed a magazine off of a table. She tried to force herself to read the magazine to keep from staring at the man. No matter how hard she tried, she kept finding herself looking over at him. She was relieved when her name was called. She got up and approached the lady that had called her name.

"Hi. I am Dr. Sullivan, please come in." Tiffany was stunned at how beautiful the lady was. Dr. Sullivan stood about 5' 11" tall. She had a nice shape, but her face was just so beautiful. She had caramel skin that was flawless, slanted eyes and sharp cheek bones. Her hair flowed down her shoulders and she had pretty, full lips.

As Tiffany followed her into the room, she noticed that Dr. Sullivan had a nice ass underneath her doctor's coat.

"Have a seat, Mrs. Smith." Tiffany took a seat on a black leather couch. Dr. Sullivan took a seat in a black leather chair, directly across from her. She held a notebook and a pen in her hand as she asked, "So what can I help you with?" Tiffany sat hesitantly. She thought that maybe it had been a bad idea to come there. Dr. Sullivan sensed her hesitation.

"May I call you Tiffany?"

"Yes,"

"Okay, Tiffany you may not know me, but you do know that I am here to help you. Now the only way I can do that is if you relax and tell me what your problem is. Remember everything that we talk about is confidential. It's strictly between you and me."

Tiffany took a deep breath and tried to relax, "I think I have a sex addiction."

"And what makes you think that?"

"I constantly have cravings to have sex."

"How often do you have these cravings?" "All the time," Tiffany answered.

"And do you act on these cravings?"

"Most of the time,"

"Is it with your husband that you act on these cravings?"

"There are others too."

"And how long has this been going on?"

"Since I was young."

"So you have been having sex with multiple partners since you were a child?"

"Yes,"

"When was the last time you had sex with someone other than your husband?"

"Last night?"

"Do you have any idea as to why you do it?"

"Because I wanted to,"

"Tiffany, how is sex with your husband?"

"What do you mean?"

"Does sex with him be satisfying to you?"

"Not really!"

"And why is that?"

"He always finishes before me,"

"So, do you think that if sex with him satisfied you, that maybe you would not seek out to have sex with other partners?"

"I don't know sometimes I need to have sex with more than one person."

"Exactly how old were you when this behavior began?"

"I was eleven,"

"I see," Dr. Sullivan said as she looked at her watch.

"Well Tiffany, we have covered a lot of ground, but unfortunately our time is up. I do have other patients that I have to see. Would you like for me to schedule you for another appointment for next Thursday at the same time?"

"Yes, I would like that." Tiffany said as she rose up out of her seat.

"Okay, I will see you next week then." Dr. Sullivan told her as she walked over and opened the door for her.

Tiffany left the office and headed for the elevators. She got on and rode down to the ground floor. When she exited the elevator and walked towards the revolving doors, someone approached her.

"Excuse me," Tiffany looked up and there stood the man she had been staring at up in Dr. Sullivan's waiting room.

"Hi my name is Marcus, I noticed that you kept staring at me upstairs. I was very flattered. I thought that maybe you were too shy to approach me, so I decided to wait for you and introduce myself. Can I ask you your name?"

"It is Tiffany,"

"So, Tiffany where are you headed?"

"Home."

"Are you driving?"

"No I am catching the bus."

"Well how about you let me give you a ride and we can stop to get something to eat and talk, is that okay?"

"Yeah I guess so,"

Marcus led the way to his car. He opened the door for Tiffany, went around to the driver's side, got in, started the car and pulled off.

"So where would you like to eat?" Tiffany don't know what made her say it, but she blurted out.

"Go to your place." Marcus raised an eye brow and smiled.

"To my place it is then." Tiffany felt nervous. She started fidgeting with her hands.

Marcus turned his music on. He looked over at Tiffany and smiled. On impulse, Tiffany reached over and put her hand in his lap.

That shook Marcus. Tiffany gently massaged his dick, through his jeans, until he became rock hard. She looked Marcus in the eyes then removed her hand and sat back in her seat.

Marcus sped up, trying to hurry and get to his house. Tiffany closed her eyes and imagined that he was inside of her. From the length of his dick, she knew that he should be able to satisfy her, if he knew how to work it and wasn't a minute man.

They arrived at his house. He got out of the car and hurried around to open the door for Tiffany. He opened the door to his house and they entered. He turned to her.

"So, what would you like?"

"Let's just go to your room."

"Uh, okay." They went upstairs to his bedroom. Tiffany immediately started to strip.

"I guess you're not shy at all." Marcus said to her as he quickly started to undress.

"You don't talk much do you?"

"Do you want to talk or fuck?" she asked as she climbed onto the bed.

"I guess we can talk later on." He climbed on the bed with her.

Tiffany assumed the doggy style position, which was her favorite. Marcus scooted up behind her, admiring her meaty ass. He took his dick and rubbed it up and down her slit, then slid up in her. He put his hands on the small of her back and fucked her with a slow rhythm. To him Tiffany's pussy felt like heaven. It was tight, wet and hot.

Tiffany rocked back and forth on her knees, going in a forward and backwards motion. She was meeting his thrust. She had her head down and began to make grunting sounds, which aroused

Marcus. "Put it in my ass!" she told him. Marcus could not believe his ears.

He quickly pulled his dick out of her pussy and positioned it at her ass hole. He tried to push his dick in but it met resistance. Tiffany turned around and put his dick in her mouth. She slobbered on it, spit on it and slurped on it. When she felt he was ready she turned back around.

Marcus tried again, and his dick sunk in. He pushed it in to the hilt. He started to slowly fuck her in her ass.

Tiffany wanted it rough. She wanted to feel like a slut. "Fuck me! Make me feel it!" she told him. Marcus let loose. He started pounding her. The slap from his thighs hitting her ass stung, but it turned her on even more. She fell flat on her stomach, and spread her legs and arms eagle. Marcus fell right along with her and kept pounding her asshole. Tiffany bit down on a pillow and gripped the bed sheets, "Oh! Ooh … Right there, bang this ass!" Marcus was covered in sweat. Every time that he raised up, it was as if Tiffany's asshole muscles were sucking him back in. "This what you want, huh? Here it comes, here it comes!" Marcus slammed into her one last time and released his load.

"Oh God!" Tiffany said as she began coming also. Her body started to convulse.

After Marcus finished, he just laid there on top of Tiffany, with his dick still in her ass. He actually dozed off for a minute.

Tiffany had to wake him. "Hey! Hey get up!"

He woke, "I'm so sorry, but you took a lot out of me."

"I need to be getting home."

"Oh, okay," they got up and got dressed. They went outside got in the car and pulled off.

Marcus turned to Tiffany, "So, when can I see you again?"

"You can't, I'm married, this was a onetime thing." Marcus got upset, about her trying to discard him like that. He drove the rest of the way in silence.

Tiffany did not care. He was lucky that she gave him what she did. She had him drop her off at the corner of her street.

Chapter 8

When Tiffany got to the house, she noticed that Kiki's car was in the driveway. She went into the house. Kiki was sitting on the couch. "Boy, why haven't I been seeing you?" "I been around?" he said dryly.

"You done got that damn car and think you're grown. You better start coming in this house, or you are going to end up living in that car!"

"Yeah, whatever," Kiki said as he got up and headed upstairs. Tiffany yelled after him, "I don't know what your problem is, but you better get it together!" she went upstairs and took a shower. After her shower, she went downstairs to prepare dinner.

At 3:30pm Donte, Angie and Keisha arrived home.

"Y'all know the drill, go wash your hands and come back down to the table."

She fixed their plates. The kids came back down and ate everyone except Kiki. When dinner was over, the kids went to do their homework and Tiffany went up to her room to watch TV.

Cliff did not come in until 11:30pm. Tiffany was still watching TV, when he came in. Cliff sat on the end of the bed, took his Timbs off and asked, "So, what happened at the doctor?"

"I got to go back next week."

"So what test did they do?"

"We just talked."

"Fuck you mean y'all just talked? What kind of test do they do talking?"

"See that's why I didn't want to tell you, I knew you would act like this."

"Act like what? I'm just trying to find out what the hell is wrong with you. So you need to start talking."

"I'm seeing a psychiatrist."

"A what?"

"A psychiatrist Cliff, you know a head doctor."

"I know what the hell a psychiatrist is, what the fuck you seeing one for?"

"I feel like I am losing my mind. Sometimes I feel like I'm not myself and I be having crazy thoughts." Cliff did not know how to react to what Tiffany had just told him. He thought to his self, "I knew she had issues, but damn." He got up off of the bed and started pacing the floor. He stopped and turned to Tiffany.

"I'm still not understanding, what it is that you're saying is wrong with you."

"I don't know what I'm saying either, Cliff. That is why I am seeing a doctor."

"Listen Tiff, I love you with all my heart. I married you despite the fact that you have four kids. That should show you that my love for you is unconditional. Now I'm going to be patient with you, but after your next visit, I hope that you will be able to give me a better understanding of what is going on with you. Do you hear me?"

"Yeah, I hear you." Cliff climbed back in the bed. It was a restless night for both of them.

Tiffany did not think that she would ever be able to tell him what her real problem was. He was a nice man and never had raised a hand towards her or her kids. She thought if he found out the truth that he might leave her and she was afraid of being alone.

34

Chapter 9

Cliff laid there fuming, he thought everything was fine. He took good care of her and her kids. Now she was telling him that she was losing her mind. What type of shit is that, he thought. He considered himself to be strong, but he felt he needed to clear his head. He got out of bed and put his clothes on.

Tiffany played sleep, she cried silently as he left out of the room. She prayed that she could get it together.

Cliff got into his car. He set there for a minute trying to clear his head. He pulled a half of a blunt out of the ashtray and lit it. When he finished the blunt, he started the car and pulled off. He drove around with no intended destination. He tried to figure out why he loved Tiffany.

He thought back to when they first met three years ago. They had met through his cousin Sheila, who was a friend of Tiffany's. He was over at Sheila's house one day, when Tiffany came over. Her smile and the sparkle in her eyes caught his attention. He was instantly drawn to her. He took her out a few times and they connected. Even after he found out that she had four kids, he still chose to pursue her.

He never thought of himself as the settling down type, but something about Tiffany pulled him in. Within six months he had moved in. Six months later they were married. He still fucked other women. He felt that it was what men did. He felt that it did not take away his love for Tiffany.

He drove around aimlessly for about an hour then headed home.

Chapter 10

The next day, Angie stood in the hallway of her school talking to Dink. Dink was supposed to be her boyfriend. Lately, he had been pressuring her to let him and his friend Jarrod run a train on her.

"So is you going to do it or not?" he asked her.

"If you care about me, why do you want me to have sex with your friend?"

"For the experience, everybody is doing it, it will be fun. Just trust me." Angie thought about it. Jarrod was attractive to her and she thought that maybe it would give her a chance to find out why her mother loved sex so much.

"Okay, but I only want you two there, no one else!" Dink couldn't believe what he was hearing. She really agreed to do it. He got so excited, that Angie had to tell him, "Calm down already." He calmed himself.

"Listen, skip out of last period and meet us at McDonald's." Angie agreed and they parted ways.

At 1:45pm Dink and Jarrod were sitting in a stolen car in McDonald's parking lot waiting on Angie.

"Are you sure she is going to do it?" Jarrod asked.

"I'm a mack, I got this." Dink bragged.

"Okay big pimping." Jarrod said with a smirk on his face.

She was still unsure about what she was about to do. She really liked Dink and did not want him to be mad at her. She crossed the street and headed to McDonald's parking lot. When she was about to go into the parking lot, a car pulled up beside her.

"Get in." Dink told her.

"Boy, who car is that?"

"Don't worry, it's all good get in." Angie opened the back door and got in.

"Hey Angie," Jarrod said.

"Hey Jarrod," was all that was said. They drove to Dink's house, quietly trapped in their own thoughts.

Once they got to the house, Dink had them enter through the side door. He led them down to the basement, which was where he slept. They entered his room and he led Angie over to the bed. She sat down with Dink sitting down next to her. He pushed her down and started unbuttoning her shirt. He then undid her pants and tried to pull them down. Angie sat up, rolled her eyes.

"I'll do it."

She stood up, took off her shirt, pants and bra, then she sat back down on the bed.

Dink quickly took off his pants and underwear and got back on the bed with her. He went straight to the act. He spread her legs and entered her. Angie did not feel a thing. She turned her head to see what Jarrod was doing. He was standing there, still fully clothed watching them.

Dink was pumping fast and breathing hard. What he was doing did nothing for her. There was no fun and no pleasurable feeling. She wondered was it going to be the same with Jarrod.

Dink's body had a spasm and he was through. He got up and turned to Jarrod.

"Go ahead dawg, it's good." then he ran up the stairs.

Jarrod smiled and started undressing. He took off all of his clothes. Angie laid there looking at his body in amazement. He had muscles bulging from everywhere. When she lowered her eyes to his penis, she almost had a heart attack. It looked like the bottom of a baseball bat. She thought that there was no way that it would fit inside of her. She felt weird because she was dry when Dink was with her, but now she was becoming moist. She realized that the sight of him was actually making her wet.

He climbed on the bed and laid next to her. He reached over and cupped one of her breast. He massaged it then put it in his mouth. Angie's body started to heat up instantly. He started rubbing his hands all over her body. Angie started to moan. She had never done that during sex.

Jarrod positioned his self between her legs. His dick was sticking up past his navel. He took his hand and used it to guide his dick to the entrance of her pussy. Angie lifted her head and looked down, "Is it going to fit?" she asked him.

"Don't worry, I got you." he spit on the head of his dick and rubbed it up and down her slit. Then he forced the head in. Angie gasped and closed her eyes. He pushed in deeper, and Angie's eyes flew open. Tears began to run down her eyes. He went deeper and she whimpered, "It hurts."

"You're a big girl, you can handle it." he told her as he pushed all the way in.

Once he was all the way in, he laid still letting her body adjust to him. Then he started to slowly fuck her. The pain started to be replaced by pleasure.

38

Angie found herself rotating her hips.

"That's it baby girl, work that pussy." Jarrod told her. Angie reached up and put her arms around his back.

Dink ran back downstairs chewing on a sandwich. When he saw how Angie was fucking Jarrod back, he couldn't believe it and got very jealous.

"Hurry up before my parents get home."

"Okay man," Jarrod said as he picked up the pace.

He started fucking Angie harder, and she reacted by fucking him back. She even called out his name, "Oh, Jarrod!" as she felt tension build up in her body. Angie made a noise that Dink had never heard before as she came for the first time in her life.

Jarrod busted off in her. Angie held onto his back trying to keep him inside of her. Jarrod kissed her on the forehead.

"We got to go, baby girl." Angie just gazed in his eyes. She thought to herself, "Now I know why my mother loves sex." she fell in love with Jarrod.

Dink was pissed, "Hurry up!" he yelled at them. He had an attitude towards Angie and did not speak to her at all on the way to drop her off.

Angie did not care. To her Dink was a little boy. Jarrod had showed her how a real man makes a girl feel. When they dropped her off, she got out of the car and said by Jarrod and walked off not paying Dink any mind.

Chapter 11

Saturday arrived and Cliff took Tiffany and the kids over to his mother's house for a family cookout. He and Tiffany had barely been speaking for the last few days. He needed to talk to someone. He figured that if he could catch his mother by herself then maybe he could talk to her and get some advice.

Everyone was in the backyard. They had card tables and domino tables going. Cliff's uncle Charlie was manning the grill. Greg was there with his girl Tonya. All the kids were playing dodge ball. Cliff's brother Ricky was deejaying.

Cliff's mother was in the kitchen making potato salad. Cliff made his way in there and sat on a stool. His mother looked at him and could see something was bothering him.

"Boy what is wrong with you?" Cliff's mother asked.

"I think I made a mistake by getting married."

"And why do you think that?"

"Because I thought I knew Tiffany, but now I'm finding out that I really don't know her."

"What do you mean, you don't know her?"

"She is keeping secrets and lying. First, she told me that she was sick, and was seeing a doctor. After her appointments I would ask her what happened and she would say that they only talked. Then she admitted that she had gone to see a psychiatrist."

"She said that she feels like she is losing her mind. She told me that she couldn't explain it, but she is going back next week, to try and get a diagnosis." Cliff told his mother.

"Oh Lord, that girl is losing her mind."

"I don't know what to do, ma."

"You stand by her, you understand me. You made vows through sickness and in health. You support her, talk to her and let her know that you are going to be there for her.

"Y'all need to start attending church. God can help that child." Cliff got up, walked over to his mother and gave her a hug.

"Thanks ma, I love you."

"I love you too, baby." Cliff went back outside. He walked over to the table where he had left Tiffany at, but she wasn't there. One of his cousins told him that she had went into the house to use the bathroom.

Greg heard what was said and crept off towards the house. One of Cliff's cousins called him over to be their spades partner. He went and joined the spades game.

β

Tiffany had just finished washing her hands, after using the bathroom. She opened the door and Greg was standing there. He pushed his way in and quickly closed the door.

"What are you doing?" Tiffany asked.

"Sit down I want you to suck my dick right quick."

"Boy, you better gone. Are you trying to get me killed?"

"Girl, doesn't anybody know that I'm up here," he told her as he unzipped his pants and pulled his dick out. Tiffany looked down at it, and then she sat on the toilet. Greg guided his dick to her mouth. Tiffany opened and received him.

Greg put his hands on her shoulders and watched as she bobbed her head up and down on his dick. Tiffany got into a rhythm, and started to enjoy giving him head. She took one of her hands and started massaging his balls.

Greg was feeling like he was in heaven when she took his dick out of her mouth and started sucking his balls. She put his balls in

her mouth and hummed on them sending a vibrating sensation through him. When she put his dick back in her mouth, he put his hands on the sides of her head to hold it still as he began fucking her in her mouth.

Tiffany enjoyed the feeling that she was getting from being fucked in her mouth. She put her hands on his ass trying to pull him into the back of her throat.

"That's the Tiffany that I like, take that dick." Tiffany closed her eyes and moaned as he fucked her face. When he was on the verge of cumming, he pulled out and told her to hold her head back and to leave her mouth open. He jacked his dick until it started skeeting. He aimed up, letting his nut shoot up in the air and rain down on Tiffany's face. Some landed in her mouth, but some also landed in her eye and on her nose.

When he was done skeeting, he put his dick back in her mouth and let her milk the last of the cum out of him. Afterwards they cleaned up and headed out of the bathroom.

Cliff's mother was coming out of her bedroom and saw them come out of the bathroom. She acted as if she did not see anything and headed downstairs.

Tiffany went back outside. Cliff saw her and called her over.

"Where have you been?"

"I was in the bathroom. Something that I ate made me sick."

"Is you good now?"

"Yeah, I feel better."

"I'm about to go and check on the kids." Tiffany told him as she walked off.

Cliff's mother sat at her kitchen table wondering what Cliff had gotten his self into. She didn't want to see him hurt so she decided not to tell him what she had witnessed. She promised herself that she was going to set Tiffany straight.

Chapter 12

It was Thursday and Tiffany was getting ready for her appointment. The rest of the week had been uneventful. One night she had gotten the urge to creep out and go up to the store, but after the close call that she had last time, she decided against it.

Cliff had started to be more attentive too, asking her if she was okay and checking on her. Tiffany left out and headed to the bus stop. She caught the bus and arrived at Dr. Sullivan's office ten minutes before her appointment.

At 9 O'clock exactly, Dr. Sullivan stepped out of her office and asked her to step in. She told Tiffany to have a seat. Tiffany sat on the same black couch, and Dr. Sullivan sat in her chair with her notebook and pen.

"So Tiffany how was your week?"

"It was okay."

"Did you refrain from having sex with someone other than your husband?"

"No, I had sex with two other people." Dr. Sullivan looked at her notes. "You say you have been experiencing this behavior since you were eleven years old?"

"Far as I can remember."

"Let me ask you this, can you remember any traumatic sexual experience that you may have had when you were younger?"

"I can't say anything before the age of eleven."

"So that's the first sexual experience that you can remember, but not necessarily the first one that you had?"

"I remember having my first sexual encounter when I was eleven."

"Do you remember that experience?"

"Yes,"

"And were you a willing participant?"

"Yes,"

"Please describe it to me."

"I was in the sixth grade. After school I went over to my friend Mona's house. We were in her room playing doctor. I was lying naked on her bed, while she examined me. She was examining my vagina, when one of her fingers slipped inside of me. Everything changed. It went from being innocent to sexual. She slid more fingers inside of me. An overwhelming feeling came over me and I found myself gyrating on her fingers. She noticed it and started moving her fingers in and out of me in a way that caused my body to react in a way that it had never done before. All of a sudden her bedroom door opened and in walked her thirteen year old brother, Mark. He saw me lying there, being fingered by his sister. He threatened to tell on us if I did not give him some. He undressed and climbed on top of me. He had sex with me while his sister stood there and watched."

"You do not feel that the threat of being told on forced you into having sex with him?"

"I think I would have had sex with him, even if he had not made the threat. I was always attracted to him."

"So your first sexual experience involved a male and female?"

"Yes,"

"And from that point on you have never had a committed relationship?"

"No,"

"How many sexual partners have you been with at one time?"

"Seven,"

"You willingly engaged in sex with seven people?"

"Yes,"

"Please explain why?"

"Shit, I don't know why. I had cut school with this guy name Mario, when I was in junior high. I guess his house was the hang out spot, because after we got there six more people showed up. Mario took me upstairs to his room to have sex. While we were up there having sex, the other six guys came and stood in the doorway and watched us, it turned me on. Mario couldn't make me cum. A lot of young guys did not know how to make a girl cum. An older guy had exposed me to the feeling of a climax. I used to chase that feeling, like a fiend would chase a high, and that day I did not cum until the fifth guy had sex with me. He was Mario's brother, Rob."

"Okay, well again that is our time. Tiffany, it is apparent that you have a sexual dysfunction. What I am trying to find out is the cause of it. I want you to think about something, and try to have an answer by our next appointment, which will be the same day and time next week. I want you to try and figure out what is it that you seek to get out of sex. You mentioned orgasms. So figure out if it is your constant need to have an orgasm, or do you think it is a mental thing, maybe the need to feel accepted. Try to figure it out and I will see you next week." she escorted Tiffany out of her office.

β

Later that night Cliff came in. He was anxious to know what she had found out. Tiffany was sitting up in bed watching TV.

"So what's the verdict?" he asked.

"I have to go back next week."

"Tiff, what kind of game is you playing. Are you going to keep stringing me along?"

"We only have an hour session, Cliff. She said that we need to talk some more before she can make a diagnosis."

"I'll tell you what, I'm going to your next appointment with you."

"No you're not."

"Oh, I can't go with you? What are you trying to hide from me Tiff?"

"I ain't trying to hide nothing."

"Then why can't I go with you?"

"Because it is something that I need to work out on my own."

"It's suppose to be us Tiff, us. I have been trying to be patient with you and trying to support you, but you continue to freeze me out. So here is the plan, you just do you and I'm going to do me."

"What do you mean by that?"

"It means that I'm going to stay out of your way. You handle yours and I will handle mine."

"That's not fair, Cliff. What I'm going through has nothing to do with you. People including you have always helped me. I need to do something on my own for a change. Why can't you just give me that?"

"I'm going to give you all the space that you need." he told her as he walked out of the room.

Cliff left the house. He decided that he would stay at his mother's place for a couple of days. He still had a room there.

β

When Cliff's mother got up the next morning, she noticed his car parked in her driveway when she was leaving for work. She wondered what had happened between him and Tiffany that caused him to spend the night at her house. She decided that when she got off of work, she was going to pay Tiffany a visit.

β

She got off of work at 5 o'clock and caught the bus over to Tiffany's.

Tiffany was upstairs when she heard a knock at the door and hurried downstairs to answer it. She was surprised to see Cliff's mother standing there when she opened the door.

"Hey Mrs. Smith, come on in." Cliff's mother walked in and took a seat. Mrs. Smith spoke, "I like you Tiffany and I thought you were a good girl, but I seen the truth. Now I'm not going to just sit back and allow you to hurt my baby."

"Mrs. Smith I have no idea about what you're talking about."

"I saw you Tiffany, with my own eyes."

"You seen me what?"

"At my house, the cookout, I saw you and Greg creep out of the bathroom together." Tiffany put a shocked look on her face. "We were just talking."

"Child I'm sixty two years old. I wasn't born yesterday. I know what y'all were doing. Greg is his first cousin. It would kill him to find out that y'all betrayed him. Now he told me that y'all were having some issues and that you are seeing a psych, whatever is wrong with you, you need to get it straight ASAP. My son loves you and your kids. He is a good man. You're not going to tear my baby apart. And I don't know why he had to sleep at my house last night, but he will be back here tonight. Y'all work this mess out. I'm too old for this shit. Do you hear me?"

"Yes ma'am."

"Now this conversation is going to remain between just us. I got to get home so I can take my insulin. You get it together." she told Tiffany as she got up and headed out of the door.

Tiffany sat there stunned. She did not know what to think. Cliff's mother had seen her and Greg. Even though she said she was not going to tell him, it still made Tiffany nervous. She knew that from then on she was going to feel uncomfortable around Cliff's mother. Also, she knew that a mother's loyalty lies with their child. At any time she could decide to tell Cliff. That made Tiffany feel trapped.

When Cliff's mother got home, Cliff was sitting on the couch moping.

"Boy, what is wrong with you? You got that damn sad look on your face."

"I'm tired, ma. This shit with Tiffany is getting ridiculous. If I continue to stay around her, I might end up putting my hands on her." "Boy! No matter what, you never put your hands on a woman. You hear me?"

"Yes ma'am"

"Now listen, it isn't always going to be sunshine. The rain comes too. And when it does, you have to be able to withstand it. What makes you a man a stronger, wiser man is going through rough times and making the right decisions. Now, you man up and take your ass home. Y'all work that shit out. Go on, now." Cliff got up and headed out the door.

Chapter 13

It was Saturday and Cliff thought that he should take Donte out to the ball park to spend some time with him. He headed up to Donte's room. He opened the door and had seen Donte quickly try to hide something under his pillow.

"What is that you put under the pillow?" Donte put his head down.

"Nothing," Cliff approached the bed and told him to move. He reached under the pillow and pulled out two baby dolls. Cliff couldn't believe it. He had thought that maybe he had hid a cigarette or a joint, but he was fifteen years old playing with baby dolls.

"Whose are these?"

"They are Keisha's."

"What the hell are you doing with them?"

"I was just playing with them."

"Boys your age doesn't play with any damn dolls. Get up, put your shoes on and let's go." Donte got up, put his shoes on and they headed out of the door.

Cliff took him to a pee wee league football game, being held at the neighborhood park. He got them some hot dogs and sodas. They found some seats on the bleachers.

Halfway through the game, Cliff took notice of the fact that Donte showed no interest in the game whatsoever. He sat there with an expressionless face. No cheering, nor excitement at all. Cliff knew that he would have to have a talk with Tiffany about him. There was no doubt in his mind that Donte was on his way to being gay, if he wasn't already. Cliff thought that maybe Tiffany should have Donte see a psych also. Since the boy had no interest in doing anything manly. Cliff decided to take him back home.

When they got there Donte headed upstairs to his room and Cliff went in search of Tiffany. He found her in the kitchen at the stove cooking.

"How are you doing?" he asked her.

"I'm okay,"

"Tiff, I think Donte might need some help."

"Why do you say that?"

"Come on Tiff, you don't notice how feminine the boy acts. I went up to his room today to get him. I was taking him to a football game with me. When I opened his bedroom door he tried to hide something under his pillow before I could see it. I went under the pillow and pulled out two baby dolls. He told me that they were Keisha's. Then I took him to the game, and he showed no interest in it whatsoever. I'm telling you, if you don't get that boy some help now, he's going to be gay."

"Donte is not going to be gay. He is just shy. He will grow out of it."

"Just shy my ass! Tiffany he is fifteen playing with baby dolls. Talk to the boy, I bet you that he doesn't even have a girlfriend."

"I will have his father talk to him."

"I ain't say shit about his father. I asked you to talk to him. You need to start paying more attention to these kids. Kiki is never here, Angie has been disappearing a lot lately and she is starting to dress too provocative for her age. I guess with all of your problems you haven't had a chance to take notice of the kids."

"That ain't fair Cliff. I do take notice of my kids. I will talk to Donte, okay?"

"Yeah, you do that." Cliff said as he angrily walked out of the kitchen.

Tiffany felt like the walls were closing in on her. It seemed as if her life was falling apart. She felt drained. She went upstairs and got into bed and instantly fell asleep.

During her sleep, she started dreaming. In the first dream, she was in Dr. Sullivan's office, and they both were naked. Dr. Sullivan had Tiffany laid out on top of her desk, with her legs spread wide open. Dr. Sullivan was in between Tiffany's legs eating her pussy.

In the dream Dr. Sullivan had convinced Tiffany that she needed physical therapy. She told Tiffany that she was going to do sexual things to her to see how her body would react. In the dream she did many things to Tiffany, from planting soft kisses all over her body to blowing into her ass hole. Everything that she did to Tiffany caused her to have an orgasm, even sucking her feet.

That dream ended and another one started. In that dream Tiffany was much younger, and someone whose face she could not see was having sex with her. He was talking to her as he was having sex with her and she could feel his hot breath on her ear.

She could not see his face, nor place his voice, but he did things to her that made her cum numerous times.

The dreams that Tiffany had were so real, that when she woke

up she felt stickiness in between her legs. She reached down and

pulled

her hand up to her face and seen that it was cum. Cliff was not in bed with her, so she knew that she had a wet dream.

She sat up and started to think about the question that Dr. Sullivan had given her. What is it that she seeks to get out of having sex? She pondered that question. All she could come up with was the euphoric feeling that came over her, whenever she would climax. It was the ultimate high. She did not feel that it was about a man, because it did not matter where her nut came from. It could come from a man, woman or her vibrator. All she wanted to do was to feel that high.

"At least I have something to tell Dr. Sullivan at my next appointment." she said to herself.

Chapter 14

Since her sexual encounter with Dink and Jarrod. Angie had become a new person. She had become sexually free. For a week straight she had cut school to have sex with Jarrod. She no longer messed with Dink.

Jarrod had introduced her to a bunch of new things. He performed oral sex on her, and then taught her how to perform it on him. He introduced her to anal sex, and though it had hurt the first time Angie grew to love it.

After sexing Jarrod for a week straight she became bored with him. She started wearing skimpy outfits and was drawing attention from many of the boys at school. Her name started ringing bells throughout the school as she became known as easy and down for whatever. She would have sex with a group of boys in their locker room or behind the bleachers in the gym.

It was like she was doing a re-enactment of her mother.

She started missing so many days in class, that she was called to the principal's office.

The principal informed her that she was suspended from school until one of her parents brought her back to explain her excessive absences from class.

Angie cried on her way home. She did not know what she was going to tell her mother. She wondered if she would be better off telling Cliff and asking him to take her back to school.

She arrived home about 11:15am. She dreaded going into the house. Not knowing what to expect from her mother, once she told her that she had gotten suspended.

She entered the house and it was quiet. She figured that her mother was sleeping late. First she thought she should just go to her room and avoid her mother, but she decided that she might as well get it over with.

She walked towards her mother's room. The door was closed, and instead of knocking she just opened it.

She was startled when she opened the door and there was Cliff's cousin Greg fucking her mother doggy style on the bed. They were facing the door, and Greg saw her as soon as she opened the door. He looked at her evilly as he fucked her mother. Tiffany had her head down, with her eyes closed. Angie gasped and tried to cover her mouth.

Tiffany heard her and her eyes flew open and she looked up and locked eyes with her. Angie started back peddling out of the room. She quickly ran to her own room, slammed the door, jumped on the bed and started crying.

Tiffany scrambled off of the bed and started putting on her clothes. She screamed at Greg, "Get out! Get your shit and get out! I told you to stop coming over here! Now look what happened!"

"Just calm down, go and talk to her, she isn't going to say shit." "That ain't the point! That's my daughter! I don't want her looking at me in a bad way!"

"Her little ass probably is fucking like crazy herself."

"If she is, it's none of your business! Now get your ass out and don't come back!"

"Bitch you better watch how you talk to me, before I tell Cliff what's really up."

"Go ahead, do it, so he can kick your ass too!"

"Hoe, I ain't scared of Cliff's soft ass, and I can show you better than I can tell you." he said as he headed out of the bedroom.

Tiffany had tried to bluff him but she was really scared to death of him telling Cliff. She ran out of the bedroom after him.

"Greg, hold up."

"Fuck that, your mouth too slick. Deal with the consequences of it." he said as he walked out the door.

Tiffany stormed back upstairs and headed towards Angie's room. She opened the door and seen Angie curled up on the bed in a fetal position crying. Tiffany wasn't concerned with her crying. She blamed Angie for the situation that she was now in. She wanted to know what she was even doing home from school.

"Get your ass up! Get up!" Still sniffling Angie sat up.

"Why in the hell ain't you in school?"

"They sent me home."

"For what dammit?"

"They say I missed too many days and that you got to take me back."

"What the hell you mean you missed too many days, heifer? You leave this house every morning to go to school, if you ain't been at school then where the hell have you been?"

"I just have been skipping some classes."

"Oh, you just have been skipping some classes. How about I skip over there and beat your ass?" she said as she approached

Angie. She reached out and grabbed Angie by the hair and pulled her off of the bed. She started hitting her with an open hand. Angie struggled to get away. Angie went from being scared to being angry.

There it was she had only skipped a few classes, but her mother was fucking her husband's cousin in their bed and she was being beat like she stole something.

Angie was the same height as Tiffany and they weighed about the same. Angie's anger gave her extra strength. She put her arms out, and with force pushed Tiffany back into the door. Tiffany's head hit the door, and she let go of Angie's head, not believing that she was fighting back.

"You little bitch. I will kill you."

"That's what you are going to have to do, if you put your hands on me again. You want to hit on me, while you have been fucking everybody behind Cliff's back."

"I still remember waking up one night, when I was younger to go to the bathroom. Your door was cracked and I looked in. You were having sex with two men at the same time. Two men, ma! Also I came home from school one day and seen you fucking Mike. Cliff's best friend, ma! Today it's his cousin, but you want to put your hands on me?"

Tiffany was taken aback. She could not believe that Angie had witnessed all those things. She started to get a migraine headache. She turned to leave Angie's room but Angie followed behind her.

"I'm just like you, ma. That's why I got suspended. I been skipping school, having sex with boys. I have been trying to find out what it is that you get out of having sex with everybody. Maybe then I will understand why I ain't got a father. There has got to be something about it that keeps you from being able to have just one man." Tiffany couldn't take any more. She went into her room, slammed the door and locked it.

Angie slid down on the floor with her head lying on the door, as she continued to talk.

"Why ma?" Why don't I have a father? Do you remember who he was? I'm going to be just like you." she said as she sat there crying.
She fell asleep in that same spot.

Chapter 15

Donte and Keisha arrived home from school. They thought that it was strange that Tiffany wasn't in the kitchen preparing dinner. The house was quiet. Together they headed upstairs. Once they came to the top of the steps they saw Angie sitting on the floor outside of their mother's room.

"Angie, get up" Keisha said. Angie opened her eyes and looked up at them.

"What's wrong Angie?" Donte asked her.

"Nothing," Angie said as she got up off of the floor.

"Y'all go to your rooms. I'm going downstairs to fix something to eat."

"Where's mommy?" Keisha asked.

"She is in the bed. She is not feeling well. Now, go ahead. I'm going to call y'all when the food is ready." They headed to their rooms. It seemed crazy that Donte was older than Angie, but next to Kiki, Angie was the most outspoken.

The rest of the night was uneventful. Angie made them some food, they ate and watched TV until it was bedtime. Tiffany never came out of her room.

The next day Tiffany woke up about seven in the morning. She had to get ready for her appointment with Dr. Sullivan. She had so much going through her mind she truly thought that she was going insane.

First, it was Kiki, then Cliff and now Angie. It seemed that everyone was turning against her. Not to mention her run in with Cliff's mother and the threat from Greg. She was going to need more than an hour with Dr. Sullivan today. She popped two Advils, and then jumped in the shower. She stayed up under the hot water for twenty minutes, trying to get the tension out of her body. She got out and got dressed figuring that she would deal with Angie when she got back.

She left the house and walked to the bus stop. On her way, she wondered if Greg had followed through with his threat. She did not think that he did, because Cliff had not stormed into the house and beat her ass. She hadn't seen him in over two days.

She caught the bus. Sitting on the bus she began to replay all the events from the past couple of days in her head. She wanted to make sure that she knew everything that she wanted to talk about. She did not want to forget anything.

After Tiffany left the house Cliff came in. He had not had a shower or a change of clothes in the past two days. He knew that Tiffany's appointments were on Thursdays at nine, so he made sure to go to the house after she had left. He had been avoiding her, fearing that he would not heed to his mother's words warning him about hitting women. He thought maybe some space is what they needed.

He entered the house, went straight upstairs and went into the bathroom. He stripped out of all of his clothes and jumped in the shower. After he finished showering, he dried off and put his clothes in the hamper. He walked out of the bathroom. Thinking that no one else was in the house, he walked out naked.

Angie had just woke up and had to use the bathroom. She left out of her room at the same time that Cliff was leaving out of the bathroom. They both looked up at the same time. Neither one spoke. Cliff stood there naked and Angie only had on her panties and a bra. Angie stared at his penis. Cliff stared at the pussy hairs that were sticking out the top of her panties. Finally he broke the spell and put his hands down to cover his self.

"Angie, why aren't you in school?"

"I got suspended until somebody takes me back." she said while still trying to stare at his penis. Cliff noticed her hard stare and quickly stepped into the room. He pushed the door up until only his face could be seen and told her to get herself together and let him get dressed. He was going to take her back to school.

"Alright," Angie said as she went into the bathroom. She used the bathroom, washed her face, brushed her teeth, then went back to her room and got dressed.

She went downstairs to make her some cereal and wait on Cliff.

Cliff was upstairs looking for a clean pair of socks, he couldn't find any in his drawer, so he opened up Tiffany's sock drawer. He went to picking through her socks and his hand hit a hard object. He dug under the socks and pulled out a long black vibrator. He reached back in and came back out with a DVD. He put the DVD into the player and turned it on. Two naked people having sex popped up on the screen. He got immediately pissed. What the hell did she need a vibrator and a porno tape for? Why was she hiding them from him?

He was realizing more and more that he didn't really know Tiffany anymore. He left the vibrator on the bed and left the DVD playing.

He went downstairs and told Angie, "Let's go." They went out, got in the car and road up to her school in silence.

β

Tiffany got to Dr. Sullivan's office. When she took a seat in the waiting room, she noticed Marcus sitting in there. He looked over at her and smiled. Tiffany gave a slight smile back. He got up and started to approach her. Soon as he stood in front of her, Dr. Sullivan called her name. Tiffany quickly jumped up, and avoided looking at Marcus as she walked into the office. She did not wait to be told to take a seat. She went and flopped down on the couch and put her face in her hands.

Dr. Sullivan grabbed her pad and pen, and took a seat. She noticed that Tiffany seemed distressed.

"So, Tiffany you look as if you have had a bad week. Do you care to tell me about it?"

"So much has happened I do not know where to begin."

"Why don't you take a deep breath, hold it, count to ten then let it out." Tiffany did as she was told. Once she was finished, Dr. Sullivan told her to close her eyes and do it one more time.

Tiffany repeated the process. Once she was done, she felt more relaxed.

"Do you feel a little better?" Dr. Sullivan asked her.

"Yes, a little bit."

"Okay then, let's start from the time that you left last week, and work your way up through the events that have taken place up to today.

"Tiffany closed her eyes and tried to put things in order in her mind. She opened her eyes, let out a deep breath.

"Okay, first my husband knows that I am seeing you and he's giving me a hard time. He wants to know exactly why I am seeing you. And since I won't tell him or let him come with me to see you, he has been very upset. We have been constantly arguing, and now I haven't seen him for the last two days."

"On top of that his mother confronted me. She knows about one of my indiscretions with his cousin. Not only that, yesterday my daughter came home from school early and caught me having sex with this same cousin. His cousin then threatened to tell my husband about us." Tiffany continued.

"After blaming my daughter for catching us and confronting her she confessed that she has been having sex with numerous guys. She told me that she is doing it to be like me. She even told me that she had witnessed me having sex on many different occasions with different men. Then ..."

Dr. Sullivan cut her off. "There is more that happened?" "Yes, a whole lot more." Tiffany answered.

"Well, let's slow down and try to work through all of this first. You have had a very busy and disturbing week. Let's start with your husband. How did he find out that you are seeing me?"

"He caught me coming into the house at two in the morning, the night before my first scheduled appointment. I tried to tell him that I had went out for a pack of cigarettes, but he said that he had been up for over a hour waiting on me. So, I told him that I was nervous about having to come see you. He did not know that you are a psych. He thought it was something that was physically wrong with me. After my first visit, he questioned me about my diagnosis. So I had to tell him the type of doctor that I am seeing."

"But you did not tell him why you are seeing me and that is putting a strain on your marriage?"

"Yes,"

"Let me ask you this. Have you discussed with your husband his sexual dysfunction?"

"No, I could never do that."

"Tiffany, one of the keys to having a healthy relationship is communication. If he is not pleasing you during intercourse, then you need to find a way to talk to him about it. Otherwise your marriage is doomed. You will forever be cheating. You see where that is getting you?"

"The cousin, now your daughter, you are playing with fire. It seems that not only do you need help, but your husband and daughter may need it also. You said that she confessed to having sex with many individuals and wanting to be like you?"

"Yes, she also blamed me for her not having a father in her life. She sat outside of my bedroom and asked me why she does not have a father. And she got suspended from school for missing too many classes."

"It is obvious that your behavior has affected her, which is typical. Kids tend to immolate their parents behavior. Often time out of frustration they will act out trying to get the attention of their parents.
How old is your daughter?" Dr. Sullivan asked.

"She is fourteen."

"She is at a transitional stage, she is turning into a young woman and trying to find herself. Her hormones and emotions are running on high. I think she may need some professional help, someone that can help her work through her issues. It does not necessarily have to be me, but she should talk to someone. So think about that, okay?" Dr. Sullivan looked at her watch, "That is our time."

"But there is more that I need to talk about."

"My appointments are set by the hour Tiffany."

"I need more than an hour, Doc. I am going through so much right now. I don't know if I can keep my sanity."

"Tiffany this is what I am going to do. I'm going to write you a prescription for one hundred milligrams of Prozac. You are to take one tablet a day. This will help you with your anxiety and depression. Also I am going to have my secretary try to set aside a two hour slot for you next week. Once she has done that, she will call you and inform you of the date and time. Now this is what I want you to do, write down everything that we did not get to talk about today, so that you don't forget them next week okay?"

"Okay,"

"Also I want you to talk to your husband. Tell him what you think is missing between y'all. He cannot fix what he doesn't know is broken. Lastly, I want you to reach out to your daughter and see if she is willing to get some help. Can you do those things?"

"I'll try,"

"Okay, you do that and I will see you sometime next week." She gave Tiffany the prescription and led her out of her office.

Tiffany headed towards the elevators only to be cut off by Marcus.

"How are you doing, Tiffany?"

"Not so good, look Marcus that was a onetime deal. I should not have done it. I am going through a lot of problems right now, and I have to go." She stepped around him and pressed the elevator button.

"Tiffany, I understand all that you are saying and I respect it. I can be a good friend. I am a good listener. Maybe I could help you. Be a good ear, a shoulder to lean on, or possibly give you advice. You look like you could use a friend." Tiffany thought about what he said. She could use a friend right about now, someone to talk to.

"You aren't just trying to fuck me again are you?"

"Tiffany, you came on to me the first time. I had no intentions of having sex with you. I was trying to get to know you. I was surprised at how forward you were, but it did not stop me from liking you as a person and wanting to get to know you." Tiffany again thought about what he was saying and realized that he was right. It was her that had come on to him.

"Okay, can you take me to the pharmacy, so that I can pick up a prescription?"

"Sure," he said as he held the elevator door open for her.

Chapter 16

Angie and Cliff were sitting up in the principal's office.

"So Mr. Smith do you know that Angie has been missing many days of classes?"

"Yes I do, Sir."

"And could you tell me why?"

"Well her mother has been very sick and because I have to work, Angie has been tending to her." Angie raised her eyebrow and looked over at Cliff. Luckily the principal did not catch it. She couldn't believe that he was sitting up there lying for her.

"Well, Mr. Smith, Angie has fallen behind on a lot of work. I'm afraid that if she continues to miss her classes that she will find herself repeating the same grade next year."

"I just got paid and hired a nurse to come by and help her mother therefore, Angie will not be missing anymore classes. Also I promise you that I will make sure that her after school hours and her weekends will be dedicated to catching up on her work. You have my word sir."

"Very well then Mr. Smith," the principal said as he stood up and extended his hand to Cliff. They shook hands, and then the principal turned to Angie, "You may return to class young lady, and I will tell you that I am counting on you."

"Thank you Mr. Harris," Angie told him as she left out of the office. She and Cliff walked back to his car.

She grabbed her book bag out of his car, and then asked him, "Why did you cover for me like that?"

"You are going through enough as it is. I don't want you missing out on anymore school. You need your education. With that being said, I put my word on you, so I expect you to do exactly what I promised him that you would do. Keep your butt in school okay?"

"Okay,"

"Now get your butt to class." Cliff took off heading back home. He felt that he needed to stop avoiding Tiffany and have a talk with her.

Chapter 17

Marcus took Tiffany to pick up her prescription and then to lunch. They talked for about an hour. Tiffany found out that he actually was a good listener and very insightful.

She felt a little better, after talking with him. He gave her his number and told her to call him anytime she felt like she needed someone to talk to. He then, drove her to the corner of her street and dropped her off.

Tiffany walked the one block to her house. She noticed that Cliff's car was parked in the driveway. She did not know if she was ready to talk to him yet. How could she explain to him, his short comings?

She entered the house and headed upstairs to her bedroom. She walked in and Cliff was sitting on the bed watching the DVD. The vibrator was lying next to him. They looked at each other.

"You want to explain this?" he asked her holding up the vibrator and pointing at the TV screen.

"Sometimes I need some me time."

"Fuck you mean you need some me time? What I don't satisfy you?"

"You always finish too fast, Cliff. You don't do it long enough for me to have an orgasm."

"So, I don't make you cum but a vibrator and porno do?"

"You rush into the act and finish too soon. You don't take your time and explore all of my spots."

"Ain't this a bitch, so when were you going to tell me this shit?"

"Actually, I was coming home to tell you right now. Dr. Sullivan just urged me today to come home and talk to you."

"So that's what you been seeing that shrink bitch about. You telling her that I can't satisfy you?"

"That's one of the things that we talked about." Cliff felt a tremendous blow to his manhood. There it was his wife was telling him that he did not please her in the bedroom. He got angry.

"Bitch, ain't shit wrong with me. You're the one with the problem. Whatever the hell is wrong with you is probably the reason why you can't get off." Tiffany dared not tell him, that she came with almost everyone except him.

"Cliff I love you, and I want our marriage to work. We can try new things, different techniques. Maybe get some Viagra or stay hard cream, so that you can do it longer."

"Bitch! I don't need shit to keep my dick hard! If your pussy was better my dick would stay up! I'm out of here!" he grabbed a garbage bag and started pulling open drawers. Pulling the clothes out and stuffing them into the bag.

Tiffany just sat on the bed crying. Cliff filled the bag up.

"I'll be back to get the rest of my shit later." then he walked out.

Tiffany walked over to the window and watched him put the bag into the trunk, get in his car and pull off.

Chapter 18

Kiki was sitting on top of his car up in Wendy's parking lot, when three teenage boys approached him.

"You're Kiki, right?" one of the boys asked.

"Who wants to know?"

"I do,"

"And who you supposed to be?"

"I'm Rick, Renee's brother."

"Okay, what's up?"

"You like playing games with girls, huh?"

"Dawg, I don't know what you're talking about. You got the wrong one."

"No, I got the right one. You are fucking my little sister and her friends, treating them like you're their pimp. You got my sister pregnant, and now you're ducking her."

"Your sister is too easy. If she gave it to me that quick, then who knows how many other niggas she gave it to?"

"You are calling my sister a hoe?" Rick asked Kiki as he walked up on him. Kiki hopped off of his car.

"Man, I ain't called her nothing, but it's whatever." Rick swung on Kiki catching him on the chin. Kiki staggered back, and then rushed Rick. He put his leg behind Rick's and tripped him, falling on top of him. Before Kiki could take advantage of the situation, the other two guys that were with Rick jumped in and started pounding on him. Rick got out from under Kiki and the three of them commenced to stumping Kiki out. They stumped him until he laid there limp on the ground. Then they proceeded to bust all of his car windows out, before they took off running.

The manager of Wendy's had already called the police. When the boys left, he and some of his staff went outside to see if Kiki was okay. When he saw that Kiki was lying there limp, he told one of his employees to call for an ambulance.

The police arrived first. They questioned the manager and got a description of the assailants while they waited for the paramedics to arrive. Kiki was finally conscious, but still laid out on the asphalt. The paramedics arrived. They stabilized him, put him on a stretcher and loaded him into the back of the ambulance. He was taken to Metro hospital and admitted to the emergency room.

Chapter 19

Tiffany was at home snooping through Donte's room. After learning that Cliff had caught him playing with dolls in his room, she was curious as to what else he may have in there.

He and Keisha were still at school. Being as though Angie was suspended from school, she wondered where she could be.

She had gone through Donte's drawers and his closet, and she had found nothing that sparked her interest. She decided to look under his mattress. She lifted it up and noticed the backs of two magazines. She felt relieved thinking that they were girly magazines. She picked one up, and upon turning it over, she was shocked to see a picture of a nude man on the cover. She picked up the other magazine and it too had a naked man on the cover.

She sat on his bed and began to flip through them. She was disgusted that they had all men in them. Some were posing nude, while others were engaging in sex with each other.

Tiffany was hit with reality. There was no more denying that Donte was more than just shy. She decided that she was going to confront him as soon as he walked through the door. She loved her kids, and now she started to realize that she had been so caught up with herself, that she had not been paying as much attention to her kids as she should have been.

One reason she got married was to give her kids a stable environment. So that they would not end up with the same issues that she has. She started feeling that anxiety again and against the doctor's instructions she popped two more hundred milligram tablets of Prozac.

The phone rang, it was the hospital informing her that Kiki had been admitted with minor injuries. She told the person that called that she was on her way. She called and texted Cliff. He did not return her call or text.

She decided to call Marcus. He answered on the first ring. She explained to him that it was an emergency and that she needed to get up to the hospital. He said he would take her so she gave him the address and hung up. Just when she hung up, Angie walked in.

"Where have you been?" Tiffany asked her.

"I was at school."

"I thought you said that you were suspended, until I took you back?"

"Cliff took me back."

"And when did you see Cliff?"

"This morning, when I got up he was here. He took me to school and talked to the principal. After they finished talking the principal told me to go back to class." Angie left out the part about Cliff lying to the principal to cover for her.

"Well you don't leave this house until I get back, you hear me?"

"Yeah, I hear you."

"Something done happened to your brother and he's in the hospital. I'm about to go up there to find out what's going on."

"Something happened to Kiki? I want to go with you."

"No! I need you to stay here and cook something to eat for your brother and sister. And Angie, I'm sorry for the way that I acted yesterday. I am going to talk to you when I get back okay?"

"Alright,"

A horn blew and Tiffany grabbed her purse and hurried out of the house.

She got into the car, told Marcus what hospital and they headed in that direction.

Chapter 20

Cliff was over Maria's house. Maria was his ex-girlfriend. Cliff had stopped messing with her, when he had gotten serious with Tiffany. Maria was still open off of Cliff. She never stopped caring for him. She had hoped that his relationship with Tiffany did not last and that he came back to her. She had missed the wild and freaky sex that they use to have.

Right then they was having sex. After Cliff left Angie's school, he called Maria and asked if he could come over and she had readily agreed. As soon as he entered the house they headed straight to the bedroom. They were naked on the bed, and Maria was giving him a blow job.

Maria was the type of girl that got excited from performing sexually. She gave head like a porno star. She sucked Cliff off as if she was performing in a movie. She also was a talker. Being Spanish she was very vocal. She said things like, "Oh Poppi, mmm Poppi Chulo," while giving him head.

Cliff stopped her from giving him head. He told her to get doggy style on the bed. He felt that he had something to prove. He eased up behind her and inserted his dick. As soon as he was in Maria started, "Oh God, yes, yes." Cliff got up off of his knees, put his feet flat on the bed and began fucking her ferociously. The sound of his balls slapping against the back of her thighs could be heard.

Cliff mumbled to his self, "Bitch got me fucked up, ain't shit wrong with me. I sling this dick." Then he started talking to Maria. "Do daddy got that good dick?"

"Oh, yes Poppi, daddy's dick is sooo ... good."

"Cum for daddy then, show daddy that he makes you cum." Maria put her head down and started bucking and then began gyrating her hips. Her hair fell over the front of her face. She started shaking her head from side to side. Her hair was flying back and forth like some helicopter blades.

She said, "I'm cumming, Poppi!" then clutched a pillow with her hands and bit into it.

Cliff hunched over her and put his arms up under hers. They looked like two dogs in heat in that position. His stomach was on her back, with his face on the side of her face as he fucked her.

"Shit!" he said as his body tensed up. He unloaded in her. He pumped so much cum into her that he thought it was at least a pint. He was hyped up. He jumped up off the bed.

"Yeah, that's what I'm talking about nigga." he walked over to the dresser and looked in the mirror at his self. He was drenched in sweat. Maria laid on the bed looking at him in amazement. He had never fucked her like that before, when they were together. To her it was like he was possessed.

He turned to her, "Did you cum?"

"That was one of the best orgasms that I ever had."

"I knew wasn't shit wrong with me." "What
are you talking about Poppi?"

"Nothing, it don't matter." he said as he started getting dressed.

"Poppi, you no leave, please stay."

"I got some business to take care of. I will get back with you as soon as I take care of it."

"Are you sure you will come back?"

"Yeah I'm sure." he said as he grabbed his car keys off of the dresser and headed out of the door.

β

Tiffany got to the hospital. She tried to get Marcus to stay in the car, but he insisted that he go in with her. She did not feel like arguing with him, so she just headed inside, with him following behind her. Tiffany approached the admittance window.

"My name is Tiffany Smith and my son Kiante McCoy has been admitted here."

"Let me check, ma'am," the receptionist said as she typed into the computer.

"Yes, he is in emergency room number four. Dr. Ford is tending to him. Please have a seat and I will notify Dr. Ford that you are here."

"Okay, thank you." Tiffany and Marcus went into the waiting area. Tiffany sat down.

Marcus said "I'm about to go to the vending machine. Can I get you something, a cup of coffee perhaps?" Tiffany needed to pop another pill, and she needed something to wash it down with.

"Yes, bring me a cup of black coffee."

"Okay, I got you!" Marcus took off in search of the machines.

A tall thin white man wearing an overcoat and glasses came into the waiting room and called out Tiffany's name.

"Is there a Mrs. Smith in here?"

"Yes, here I am." Tiffany responded as she stood up and approached him. He extended his hand.

"Hi I'm Dr. Ford. You are Kiante's mother is that right?"

"Yes I am,"

"Well, you have a tough son Mrs. Smith. It seems that he had an altercation with several other individuals. He suffered a concussion and a few lacerations. But as I said he's a tough boy, so he will be okay."

Marcus came up along the side of Tiffany. He handed her the cup of coffee. Dr. Ford extended his hand to him, again introducing his self, "I'm Dr. Ford, are you Kiante's father?"

"No, no I'm just a friend of the family."

"Well, if you two will follow me, I will take you to Kiante." Tiffany and Marcus followed Dr. Ford down the corridor and through a set of double doors. They turned into the first room on the right.

Kiki was sitting up on the bed, being tended to by a nurse. Tiffany looked at his face. She seen that his left eye was black and the whole right side of his face was swollen. He held an ice pack in his hand. He looked up at his mother and Marcus as they walked into the room. He did not speak.

Tiffany went to him, "Are you alright?"

"Yeah I'm straight."

"Who did this to you?"

"It doesn't matter. I'm going to handle it."

"Boy, what do you mean you're going to handle it?"

"Just what I said, I'm going to take care of it."

Dr. Ford reentered the room and handed Kiante a bottle of pain pills. He told him to take two every four hours. He then turned to Tiffany, "Mrs. Smith if you could sign these papers please for insurance purposes he can be free to go." Tiffany signed the papers and they headed out of the hospital.

Kiki kept looking at Marcus, wondering who the hell he was. He followed them to Marcus's car and got into the back seat. They pulled out of the parking lot, and Kiki spoke.

"So you got another one ma?"

"Another what boy?"

"Another boyfriend?"

"No, I don't have a damn boyfriend."

"Who the hell is he then?"

"A friend of mines."

"Then he is your boyfriend."

"Stop trying to be smart Kiante. We will talk when we get home."

"I ain't going home."

"Boy, your bringing your ass home."

"I'm going to get my car first, before somebody steals it."

"Where is your car at?"

"It's in Wendy's parking lot on a 123rd." Tiffany turned to Marcus. Before she could say anything he said, "I know where it is."

Marcus drove to Wendy's, and pulled into the parking lot. Kiki's car sat there with all the windows broken out. Kiki saw his car and said, "I am going to kill those niggas."

"Kiki, you ain't going do nothing but get your but in that car and drive home. We are going to follow you." Tiffany told him.

Kiki climbed into his car, started it up, and then pulled out of the parking lot with Marcus following behind him.

Chapter 21

Once Cliff got in his car and checked his messages, he seen that Tiffany had texted him with 911 and also left a message on his phone. He dialed the house, and Angie answered the phone, "Hello?"

"Angie where is your mother?"

"She went up to the hospital something happened to Kiki."

"What do you mean something happened to Kiki?"

"That's all she told me, was that something happened to him. She told me to stay here and cook while she went up there."

"Do you know what hospital she went to?"

"No,"

"Okay, I am on my way over there. If your mother calls you before I get there, ask her what hospital she is at."

"Okay," Angie said then hung up the phone.

Cliff couldn't figure out, what could have happened to Kiki. He did know that Kiki sold dope on the low. That was how he bought his car. He thought that maybe somebody had tried to rob or jack him.

He sped up, heading towards the house.

β

Donte and Keisha came in from school. Angie told them to take their book bags up to their rooms, wash their hands then come back downstairs to eat.

They headed upstairs. Donte entered his room and on top of his bed were his two magazines. He knew that someone had been in his room because he had the magazines hid under his mattress. Someone knew his secret. He wondered who it could be.

He felt that honestly he was tired of hiding. He had been trying to be something other than what he truly was. He felt angry and confused because he had no one to talk to. For the last two years he had been in an identity crisis. Every day he found himself becoming more and more attracted to boys. He felt conflicted inside.

Neither his sisters nor his brother knew what he was going through. He did not know how to tell his mother. He was getting fed up. Now that his secret was out he thought that maybe he could finally be himself. If his family would accept him unconditionally, then he would have a heavy load lifted off of his shoulders.

He put the magazines in a different hiding place, and went downstairs. When he sat down at the kitchen table. He asked Angie if she had been in his room.

"No why?"

"Never mind," he thought, "Well, that eliminates her. Keisha had been at school with me. That leaves mommy and Kiki." He figured that he would have to wait and see who confronts him about the magazines.

Chapter 22

Three cars turned onto Tiffany's street right behind each other. Kiki pulled his car into the driveway. Marcus pulled his car to the curb in front of the house and Cliff pulled into the driveway behind Kiki.

Everybody exited the cars. They all looked around at each other. Kiki looked from his mother to Cliff, shook his head and headed up the steps, into the house.

Cliff stood there looking at Tiffany and Marcus. Tiffany turned to Marcus.

"Thanks, I have to go." Marcus nodded his head, got back in his car and pulled off.

Tiffany started walking up the driveway. When she went to walk past Cliff, he reached out and grabbed her arm, "Who was that nigga, Tiff?"

"Somebody that took me up to the hospital to get Kiki."

"Oh, he just somebody, huh?"

"Why does it matter, I texted you and called you, but you returned neither. My baby was in the hospital and I needed to get up there to see what was going on!"

Cliff realized that he was fucking Maria, when she was calling him. He felt bad, but still wanted to know what was up with that dude.

"So, you and him, are y'all messing around?"

"No Cliff, we are not messing around. Now let me go in here and find out what happened to Kiki."

They walked into the house together. Angie, Donte and Keisha were sitting at the kitchen table eating.

Cliff stopped in there with them.

"What's up Keisha?"

"Hey Cliff,"

"Everything good with school, Angie?"

"Yeah it's good."

"Donte, what's up with you dawg? You good, little man?"

"Yeah I'm fine."

"All right, y'all." Cliff said and headed upstairs.

Donte eliminated Cliff from being the one that found out his secret. That left only one person, Tiffany. Why hadn't she said anything?

Chapter 23

Tiffany went up to Kiki's room. She stepped in, and he was lying on his back on his bed with his arms folded behind his head.

"Kiki who were those boys that jumped you?"

"What does it matter to you? You don't care."

"Boy is you crazy. What the hell you mean I don't care? What would make you say something like that?"

"Evidently I was a mistake to you. You didn't mean to have me. If you did you would know who my father is. You gave up looking for him because it ain't important to you."

"You have a father, you have Cliff."

"Fuck Cliff! That nigga ain't my daddy." Cliff was standing in the doorway the whole time and heard Kiki's comment. After hearing how Kiki felt about him he spoke up.

"I'm sorry that you feel that way Kiki. I would never try to take the place of your real dad, but I do love you as if you were my own son." Kiki just looked at him, with a hard stare.

Cliff continued, "I know that your mother has made some mistakes in the past and that has evidently caused you some pain, but there is no need for you to be disrespecting your mother. She truly loves you and I know that for a fact. I suggest that you and her work through your problems. I'm about to go, if you need anything or need help with your car call me, all right?"

"Yeah alright,"

Cliff walked out of the room. Tiffany stepped out behind him and pulled Kiki's door shut.

"Thanks Cliff."

"You are welcome."

"Are you coming back tonight?"

"No, I ain't ready for all that. Get yourself together, so that you can help your kids get themselves together. They are hurting and you are the cause of it." Cliff went downstairs and left out of the house.

Tiffany stepped back into Kiki's room. He was sitting up. She sat down on the end of his bed.

"Kiki I know that I haven't been the best mom, but I do love you with all of my heart. If I knew that knowing who your father is meant that much to you, I would have never given up the search for him. I will start the search again but please don't hate me. I could not bear that. Do you need any more ice for your face?"

"No, I'm good."

"Get some rest then." Tiffany told him as she got up off of his bed and headed out of his room.

Once in the hall, she figured that she might as well go and talk to Donte too. She turned and headed towards his room. She opened his door and found him sitting on his bed openly flipping through one of the magazines.

He looked up, saw her and did not even try to hide the magazine.

"You want to talk about it?" Tiffany asked him.

"I don't care."

"Are you gay?"

"I haven't had sex with a boy, but yes I am attracted to them."

"What about girls?"

"What about them?"

"You don't have any interest in them?"

"Their cool as far as being friends with, but I'm not attracted to them."

"So what are your plans Donte?"

"I'm just tired of hiding myself from everybody. I feel alone and depressed. I just want to be who I am, and be accepted by those that matter to me. Do you love me ma?"

"Of course I love you. Why would you ask that?"

"So now that you know what is really going on with me, can you accept and support me?"

"Donte, I may have never dealt with this type of situation before, but one thing is certain, my love for you is unconditional. You are my son and I am going to support you no matter what! Now it is your peers and other people that you are going to have to worry about. Can you handle the ridicule that you are going to have to face in school and out in public?"

"I would rather deal with that, than to keep hiding who I am."

"Well, look I am seeing a doctor for some issues that I am having. If you think you need to talk to a professional. I can see about getting you an appointment. So you let me know, okay?"

"Okay, thanks mom." Tiffany turned to walk out of the room.

"Uh ma?" She turned back around.

"Can I have a hug?"

Tiffany smiled, "Sure you can have one."

She walked back over to the bed and squeezed him.

"I love you, Donte."

"I love you too, ma."

They let go of each other and Tiffany headed out of the room. Back out in the hallway she decided that she might as well end the night by talking to Angie.

She went to her room and opened the door. Angie was curled up asleep. Tiffany thought about waking her up, but she looked so peaceful sleeping that she decided that she would wait until she came home from school the next day.

Chapter 24

Tiffany went and took a hot shower, then went into her room and popped two more Prozac tablets. They seemed to have a calming effect on her. She climbed into bed and thought about what all had transpired. In the past she never really thought about the consequences of her actions. She never thought that her behavior would affect other people. Now she was realizing that her behavior was definitely affecting her kids. It was even affecting her marriage. She was hoping that Dr. Sullivan could give her answers soon.

She soon fell asleep and the dreams began. In the first dream, Tiffany was fourteen. She had skipped school with two other girls name Felicia and Mary. They had taken her over to Jerry's house. Jerry was about nineteen or twenty. He had two of his friends over there, who were about his same age. They were smoking and drinking. They also had music playing. It was a party setting. The guys passed around the drink and smoke.

Tiffany really did not drink or smoke, but to fit in she joined in on the activities. She took a shot of hard liquor that burned as it went down her throat. Then she took one of the joints and puffed on it. One of the guys saw how she was puffing on it wrong.

"Hey, you're wasting it. Come over here." He took the joint from Tiffany.

"I'm going to give you a shotgun. I'm going to put this in my mouth and blow the smoke out of the back in and you are going to suck it in and hold it for as long as you can before you let it out." He took the lit part of the joint and put it in his mouth. He blew the smoke out of the back end. Tiffany sucked in the smoke until she couldn't take any more. She held the smoke in until she started to feel lightheaded. She had no idea that the joint was laced with PCP.

All three of the girls were on cloud nine. They were high beyond comprehension. They did not even understand what they were doing, when Jerry had them perform sexually with each other. They giggled as the three men took turns with them. They even inserted foreign objects inside of them.

Suddenly Tiffany's dreamed switched. Now she was even younger. Someone with a familiar voice was having sex with her. He was hurting her. She felt pain as he penetrated her.

"Stop it, it hurts." she said.

"Don't worry, the pain will go away." A voice told her. Tiffany was crying, but the person continued to have sex with her. She could not see the person's face, but his voice sounded very familiar. During the dream Tiffany got older. The faceless person continued to have sex with her as she grew older. The sex with the faceless person had changed. It went from hurting to feeling good as time went on. There came a time when Tiffany's body would crave for the faceless man to appear. The times that he did not appear Tiffany would have sex by herself using her fingers or other objects trying to reach that climax that she would get from the faceless man.

Chapter 25

Tiffany woke up popped another Prozac pill and started to get ready for her appointment. She had a lot of things that she wanted to get off of her chest. Today, she was supposed to have a two hour session. She was hoping to be able to get everything out. After getting dressed, she went downstairs, made herself an egg sandwich and a cup of coffee. Then, she headed out of the house to the bus stop.

She caught the bus, and arrived at the office building at nine on the dot. She caught the elevator upstairs and entered the office. She approached the receptionist, "I'm here for my appointment."

"Okay, please have a seat. Dr. Sullivan should be with you any moment."

Tiffany went to have a seat, but before she could sit down Dr. Sullivan called her name. Tiffany hurried into her office and took a seat.

Dr. Sullivan grabbed her notepad and pen and took a seat. "So, Tiffany did you do the things that I asked you to do?"

"Yeah, I did it." she said as she pulled a folded piece of paper out of her pocket.

"Well then, let's start off where we left off at last week. You can take your time we have a two hour session."

"I don't know so much has happened in this past week. It's like my life is moving at the speed of sound."

"Has the Prozac been helping you?"

"A little, but it has not stopped things from occurring in my life.
Also I only have a few pills left."

"How is that? I gave you a prescription for a month's worth."

"I've had to take more than one sometimes."

"That is not good, Tiffany. Taking too much of a dose of medication at one time could be harmful to you."

"If I don't get enough I could be harmful to myself."

"How about I give you a new prescription and raise your dosage to say one hundred fifty milligrams, will that be okay?"

"We can try it."

"Okay, so let's begin. Let me see where we were last week." Dr. Sullivan started flipping through her notes.

"Okay, here we are. We left off last week talking about your daughter, who you said had been suspended from school, and blamed you for her not having a father. So did you get a chance to talk to her and see if she wanted any professional help?"

"So much has happened in the last week that I haven't had a chance to talk to her, but I did apologize for the way I acted with her."

"Is she back in school?"

"Yes, my husband took her back."

"And how are things with him?"

"Not good, he found a vibrator and a porno DVD that I had stashed in my drawer."

"And he was mad about that?" Dr. Sullivan asked

"Yeah, and the fact that I told him that he doesn't please me."

"How did he react when you told him that?"

"Shit, he got so mad. He told me that I'm the one with the problem, not him."

"So he reacted negatively?"

"Very, also I haven't seen him in the last two days. He told me that he was giving me my space to get myself together."

"Are you okay with that?"

"Not really, but it is what it is."

"Okay, let's go to the things that we did not get a chance to talk about last week."

"Well I had these weird dreams. I even had another one last night."

"And what type of dreams are they?"

"Sexual dreams,"

"Okay, what happens in these dreams?"

"Well the first one is embarrassing. It was me and you having sex right here in your office on that desk."

Dr. Sullivan stopped jotting down notes and looked at Tiffany for a minute.

"So how many times have you had that dream?"

"Just once,"

"And what were the other dreams about?"

"I was having sex with a person with no face. It's like I knew the person and their voice sounded familiar, but I couldn't see their face."

"And how many times have you had that dream?"

"The first time was the same night that I had the dream about you. Then I had it again last night."

"How old were you in those dreams?"

"I was young, but I cannot tell exactly what age I was."

"And the person in the dream is familiar to you?"

"It's like I know him, but don't know him. It's weird and hard to explain. Last night I saw us having sex on many occasions over a period of time. It went from being very painful to feeling good. I even started craving to have sex with him."

"Tiffany about this first dream, sometimes dreams evolve from suppressed thoughts. Sometimes things that we think about in our mind, but do not act on come out in our dreams. I feel that is what happened with the dream that involved me. Do you think that could be true?"

"I guess, when I first saw you I was attracted to you."

"Now, also we tend to repress some traumatic experiences. We bury them into our subconscious and sometimes those things surface through our dreams. Your mind could be fighting to keep the memory suppressed. That is probably why you cannot see the person's face. The person that you see in this dream may be the key to solving why you have a sexual addiction." Tiffany perked up.

"Are you for real? If I can figure out the person in the dream, then
I can figure out why I am so addicted to sex."

"That is a possibility, you could be suppressing a traumatic experience that could be the root of your problem."

"So how can I see the face?"

"Well, we could try hypnosis. I do not perform it, but I have a comrade who does. I could see about lining you up an appointment, if you would like."

"Yes, please do that."

"Okay, now that we have gotten that out of the way, let's move forward. So what happened during the last week?"

New Flavor Books

"I do not know where to start."

"Try chronologically. Go in order in which the events occurred."

"Well I told you that my daughter blames me for her not knowing her father, now my oldest son Kiante has also confronted me about not knowing his father. He even told me that I do not care about him. My other son Donte just told me that he is attracted to men. Shit! The only one that seems normal is my youngest daughter Keisha."

"Does she have a relationship with her father?"

"Not really, but she does know him."

"So none of your kids have a relationship with their fathers?"

"No they don't."

"Tiffany kids growing up without a father or a mother in their lives, tend to go through emotional difficulties. To them a necessary element is missing from their lives. They try to figure out why and sometimes it progresses from frustration to anger. The anger can be directed in different directions. Towards people that they know, people that they don't know and sometimes even at themselves. Some children may exhibit self destructive behavior. blaming themselves as the reason that their parent is missing from their lives. They feel as if they did something wrong. You may need to get each of your children into individual counseling, even the youngest. Even though she is not showing any signs right now, they could develop later on. So it would be better to get her seen right now."

"Shit, I'm not rich. I can't afford to pay for all my kids to go to counseling."

"Tiffany you can get it done through school, through welfare or other programs out there. You just have to seek them out. I will give you some referrals. I will have them for you at our next session. Also, 97

I will see about scheduling the hypnosis. My receptionist will call you and inform you of the date and time for that appointment. Now let me write out the new prescription for you. Tiffany please stick to the proper dosage." "I will,"

"So I will see you back next Thursday." Tiffany got up and Dr. Sullivan led her out of the office.

Chapter 26

The next day when Donte woke up, he felt a new sense of freedom. Today he felt that he would be himself. When he went to join the girls for their trek to school he let his feminine side show. He even mimicked a girl's way of talking.

"Hey y'all," Angie and Keisha looked at each other and laughed.

"Meet your new sister, Donna." he said putting his hands on his hips.

Keisha put her hand over her mouth. She could not believe that Donte was acting like a girl. It did not surprise Angie. She always felt that Donte had too many feminine ways. Brother or sister she loved him and would not judge him. She thought that his biggest challenge was going to be Kiki. Kiki might not even allow him to come into his room anymore.

They all sat together when they got on their school bus. Once they got to school they parted ways and Donte was on his own.

β

At lunch time he entered the cafeteria and sat at the table where the gay boys and girls sat. Some people at the table he had classes with. They didn't hide who they were, so he knew that they were gay.

They did not know he was gay.

The group looked at him when he sat at the end of the table. They whispered among each other. Then one boy got up out of his seat and approached Donte.

"You ready to be yourself, huh?"

"I guess you could say that." Donte replied.

"My name is Kris. Come on down here, so that I can introduce you to everyone."

Donte grabbed his tray and got up. He followed Kris down to the middle of the table. They made room for him to sit down and Kris started making all the introductions.

Donte learned everybody's name and they sat and gossiped during the whole lunch period. After lunch ended Donte got up to head to his next class. One of the boys that were sitting at the table with them approached him.

"What are you doing after school?" "Nothing,"

Donte replied.

"Why don't you come over to my house? We can help each other with our home work." Donte knew that the boy was coming on to him.

"What is your name again?"

"It's Eric,"

"Okay Eric, where should I meet you?"

"What is your locker number?"

"It's 115,"

"Just wait for me at your locker when school lets out."

"Alright," Donte told him, and then they parted ways.

Donte thought about Eric for the rest of the day. He wondered what was going to happen later at Eric's house. He found Eric attractive. He had a thuggish appearance and nobody would guess him to be gay. Donte anticipated school letting out.

After school, Eric met him at his locker and together they caught the bus to Eric's house.

They went up to Eric's room to do their homework. Within a half hour they sat their books down and let nature take its course. When Donte left Eric's house, he was truly a new person and there was no turning back.

Chapter 27

Angie had been waking up feeling sick for the last couple of days. She kept having the urge to vomit. She thought that it might be a stomach virus at first, but after taking some antibiotics and still feeling sick, she figured that it had to be something else. Then she realized that her period was four days overdue. She knew that if she was pregnant, that she was going to be in a world of trouble.

She had no idea who the baby's father could be. She had had sex with so many boys in the same timeframe. Some of the boys that she had sex with she didn't even know their names. Also, she had to worry about how her mother would react. The more she thought about it, she was following in her mother's footsteps. So how mad could her mother get.

"Maybe I could tell Cliff. He could get me an abortion and my mother would never know." she thought. She wondered if she could trust Cliff that much. She realized that she had no choice but to trust him and decided that she would call him later.

β

Kiki got his car windows fixed. He also bought his self a .38 revolver for eighty dollars. He vowed revenge on the boys that jumped him. He staked out Renee's house three nights in a row.

On the third night around eleven o'clock Renee's brother and another person were sitting on the porch. Kiki cut his lights and drove slowly towards the house. Once he was directly in front of it, he stuck his arm out of the window and started shooting. Renee's brother got hit twice. He was shot once in the side of his face and once in his chest. The other person was not hit. He jumped over the side of the porch when the shooting started.

When the gunshots stopped Renee ran over to her window. She looked out and seen a car that looked like Kiki's speed off with no lights on. Her mother and father rushed out onto the porch. Renee's brother was lying sprawled out gasping for air. His mother was screaming and yelling. His father tried to get a hold on the situation begging her to calm down.

Rick's friend came from behind the house where he had been hiding. Tears streamed down his face as he watched Rick gasping for air.

Renee ran out to the porch,"I called for an ambulance!"

His father did not think that he would survive if they waited for an ambulance.

"Grab his legs! We got to get him into the car!" his father told Rick's friend. His father lifted his upper part of his body and his friend lifted up his bottom half. Renee opened the back car door, they loaded Rick into the back seat and drove to the hospital.

When they arrived at the emergency room, Renee hopped out of the car and ran inside for help. Within minutes paramedics rushed outside with a gurney. Rick was unconscious with a weak pulse. They loaded him on the gurney and rolled him through the doors. The emergency room doctor conducted a quick evaluation and ordered that he be rushed to surgery immediately.

The hospital contacted the police, who showed up to question the family about the incident.

Renee told them that she thought that the car that was involved in the shooting belonged to a guy that she used to mess around with.

The police requested that she be brought down to the station to be interviewed.

"We are not leaving this hospital until I find out the status of my son." her father said.

"Do you think that we could interview her out in the police car?" The police officer asked.

Her father agreed to that and Renee followed the officers out to their car. They put her in the front passenger seat. The officer that was going to conduct the interview got into the driver's seat, while the other officer stood outside of the car.

"What is your name?"

"Renee,"

"Okay Renee, you said that you think that the car used in the shooting belongs to an old boyfriend of yours?"

"Yes,"

"And why would your old boyfriend want to harm your brother?"

"They got into a fight about me."

"Okay and what is your old boyfriend's name?"

"Kiante McCoy."

"What did Kiante get into it with your brother about?"

"Because he got me pregnant and then stopped talking to me."

"Did they get into a physical altercation?"

"Yes, Kiante ended up having to go to the hospital."

"Do you know where Kiante lives?"

"No, but he goes to John Hay High School."

"One last question, did you see the face of the shooter?"

104

"No, I only saw the back of the car leaving."

"I'm going to need your phone number and address." she gave the information to him.

"Okay you can go back and join your family. If we have anymore questions we will contact you."

Renee climbed out of the car and headed back into the hospital.

Chapter 28

Even after Cliff's episode with Maria, he still did not feel validated. He still needed to prove himself. He wanted to know that he could please more than one woman. He convinced Maria to have a threesome. At first she refused because she was very possessive. But Cliff gave her the ultimatum that he wasn't going to mess with her anymore if she did not partake in one, she gave in.

He even had her recruit one of her friends. She picked her friend Stacey, because she knew that Stacey was wild and free. Stacey was usually down for anything. One day she had Stacey come over to the house when Cliff wasn't there.

"Mamacita, I need a favor."

"What is it?"

"Cliff keeps pressing me to have a threesome with him. He said that's every man's fantasy, and that he has yet to experience it. He asked me to pick the person. I'm picking you because I trust you."

"Girl, that's some deep shit you're asking me. You're my girl and all, but I don't know about that one. Plus, I ain't into that girly girl shit."

"It won't be any of that. Plus, we are both clean and we are all grown. I'm asking you as a friend to do me this one favor. I will forever remain in your debt. This is my chance to win him back."

"You really care about him like that?"

"I love that nigga."

"I can't see myself having to prove my love to a nigga by letting him have sex with another woman. Hey, it's your life not mine. I'm going to do it for you, but tell that nigga he's got to wear a rubber and that he better keep his mouth shut. I do have a boyfriend and ain't trying to have to cut somebody up."

"Thank you girl, thank you so much."

"So when do you want to do this shit?"

"How about tomorrow night?"

"Girl I'm going to need to be drunk to do this shit. You tell that cheap ass nigga that he got to take us out for drinks and that the drinks are on him."

"I got you, come over tomorrow about seven and we will go down to the bar."

"Okay girl, if there is a change of plans call me." Stacey said as she got up and headed towards the door.

As soon as Stacey left, Maria called Cliff. His phone started to vibrate, and he pulled it off of his hip. He looked at the number and seen that it was Maria. He thought that she must have made it happen.

"Hello?"

"What's up, baby?"

"I'm out here getting this paper, what's up?"

"Well, I got what you wanted set up for tomorrow night with my friend Stacey. She wants to go out for drinks first to get loose is that cool?" Cliff tried to contain his excitement.

"Yeah that's cool."

"So are you coming here tonight?"

"Yeah, after I finish getting this paper, I will be there."

"Okay then, bye" Cliff was hype. Stacey was a bad chick. Cliff's dick got hard just thinking about Stacey. She was Spanish too. She only stood at 5' 2" but her body was stacked. If you put her next to Maria, she makes Maria look like a six. He couldn't wait for tomorrow to come. That night when Cliff went to Maria's house they had sex.

"Are you going back to your wife?"

"Why are you asking me that?"

"Because, I don't want to go all out for you, and then you leave me and go back to that bitch."

"You are not going all out for me, and I don't plan on leaving you. Now I do have some things that I need to work out. I am already stressing, so don't add to it. We have been having fun together, let's keep it like that."

β

The next day, Cliff and Maria were sitting in the living room watching TV when the doorbell rang. Maria got up off of the couch and went and opened the door. Stacey stood there with a smile on her face. She stepped in and headed to take a seat, but Cliff stopped her, "Let's roll, we are going to the bar." Cliff did not want to waste any time. The quicker he got them drunk the faster they could get it in, he figured.

They went to Theo's, a little bar that catered to older clientele. They all ordered drinks on Cliff. Stacey chose Tequila, Cliff picked straight shots of Hennessey and Maria chose Remy Martin. Cliff went over to the jukebox and put in a few quarters, then selected a few

108

songs. He then went back over to join Maria and Stacey at the table in the corner.

He sat there nodding his head to the music while the girls chatted. They drank about four rounds of drinks and had loosened up. Stacey spoke, "Cliff you think your man enough to handle both of us? Come on lets go big cowboy." she said drunkenly.

They headed out to the car. All three of them got into the front seat, with Stacey in the middle. "Two for one," Stacey giggled.

"We are going to be hot tamale tonight. Is your dick big Cliff?" Stacey asked then put her hand in his lap. Cliff almost crashed. The car swerved. He was shocked at her forwardness. He told her, "Chill out until we get to the house." Stacey moped, "You are no fun, I hope you are not scared." Cliff thought to his self, "I'm going to show these bitches."

He pressed down on the gas pedal, so that he could hurry up and get to the house. Once they got to the house, they entered and headed straight for the bedroom. Stacey started undressing as soon as they got inside of the house. By the time they reached the bedroom, Stacey was down to nothing but her panties and bra.

Maria looked at her body, and then hoped that she wasn't making a big mistake. She had not taken in the fact of how beautiful Stacey was. She had watched episodes of Jerry Springer before where a couple had engaged in a threesome with their friends only to have things go haywire with the couple afterwards.

She looked over at Cliff, who was already undressing and knew that there was no turning back. She started undressing also.

Stacey sat on the bed and called to Cliff.

109

"Come here, big boy." Cliff walked over to her. Stacey examined his dick. She twisted up her lips as she looked at it. She reached out and put it in her hand to measure the length and the girth. Afterwards she let it go and looked at it, like she was disgusted with it.

Drunkenly she laughed, and then said, "Girl, you willing to do whatever for this little shit? I hope he knows how to work his tongue, because that little shit ain't going to do nothing for me." she spoke as if Cliff wasn't even in the room.

Cliff got the urge to smack her. He said, "Bitch, you're drunk. I'm going to show you what's up with this dick." Stacey smirked and scooted back on the bed.

"Bring it on little man." Cliff climbed onto the bed with her.

"No … No … No! Put a balloon on it oops! I mean put a rubber on it." Stacey said wickedly.

Maria did not know what to do or say. Things were not going as according as planned. There was not going to be any fun. Maria tried to defuse the situation.

"Don't pay her no mind, baby she is drunk. Mommy is ready for you."

"No, I'm going to show this bitch!" he said while putting the rubber on.

Stacey giggled, "I may be drunk, but I ain't blind. Then again I might need glasses to see that little mother fucker."

Cliff jumped on the bed and roughly grabbed her legs bending them back to her chest. He entered her. Sticking his dick in her was like sticking a small stick in a bowl of soup. It was like swimming in the ocean. He fucked Stacey hard and she just laughed at him.

"Is that it Poppi?" she teased him.

110

He was trying to concentrate, but she kept making faces, taunting him. To keep from having to look at her face he flipped her over and started fucking her doggy style. Stacey turned her head around.

"Nothing Poppi, I feel nothing."

Cliff figured that he knew what to do. He pulled his dick out of her pussy and slammed it in to her asshole. To his surprise it went in easily. He just knew that he would be able to cause her pain, by fucking her in the ass. He found out that her asshole was just as big as her pussy.

When she looked back at him and laughed again, he couldn't take it. He got up off of her. He turned and called Maria over to the bed. Maria stood with her arms folded across her chest. She also had tears running down her face.

"What is wrong with you?" Cliff asked her.

"You are crazy, you do not care about me."

"What the hell are you talking about?"

"This was supposed to be fun. We were supposed to do it together. You were so into trying to prove yourself to her that you forgot about me. This has turned into a nightmare."

"Shit, don't blame me, your drunken ass girl messed it up."

Stacey cut in, "Pee wee Herman messed it up. Let that little dick nigga go, girl. You can do better."

Cliff got mad all over again, "You know what? Fuck both of y'all bitches, I'm out." He put his clothes on and stormed out of the house.

Chapter 29

Since Tiffany's last doctor's visit, she had been trying to have the same dream again. She was hoping to finally see the person's face, who had been having sex with her in her dreams. Either that or she wanted to try and identify the voice. She wondered if it really was possible that something had happened to her when she was a kid, and that it was buried in the back of her mind.

She started thinking back to her childhood. She remembered it as being pretty normal. It was as if there were blank periods where she couldn't remember things. She did remember that it was just her, her mother and her two brothers. Raymond was her older brother by three years. Then she had Robbie, who was one year younger than her. She remembered being closer to Robbie, than she was to Raymond, possibly because of the age difference.

Tiffany and her mother had never really been close. Tiffany never really understood why they had not been close. She always yearned to have that mother and daughter relationship, that a daughter is suppose to have with their mother, but she never got it.

Tiffany had to learn how to be a woman, out in the streets. Coming up her mother never gave her any pep talks. Not about boys, sex, or even about periods. When she found out that Tiffany was having periods, she just bought her a box of tampons and told her to put them on. She did not explain to her the reasons that she had them nor did she explain the cycles in which they came.

Tiffany thought that maybe if something did happen to her as a kid, then maybe her mother could give her some insight. She had the urge to call her mother, but figured that it might be best to talk to her face to face. She decided that she was going to pay her mother a visit the upcoming weekend.

The kids were asleep and she was up in her room, when she heard banging at her front door. She went down to the bottom of the steps and yelled, "Who is it?"

"It is the police, open up. We need to talk to you." Tiffany went to the door and opened it. There stood two plain clothes policemen.

"Are you Kiante McCoy's mother?" one of the officers asked her.

"Yes I am, why?"

"We have reason to believe that he may have been involved in a shooting that has left a young man in the hospital fighting for his life."

"I don't believe that Kiante had any involvement in no shooting."

"Well, we would like to talk to him so that we can make that determination."

"He ain't here."

"And when was the last time that you saw him?"

"A few days ago,"

"So have you had any type of communication with him in the last few days?"

"No I have not."

"Okay, well I'm going to leave you my card. Please have him get in touch with us. There has been an armed and dangerous bulletin issued against him. To prevent any harm from coming to him or our

officers, he needs to come in on his own." the officer handed
Tiffany a card and they left.

Chapter 30

Tiffany sat down on the living room couch and started crying. All she could think about were Kiki's words, "I'm going to deal with them." She picked up the phone and called Cliff. His phone went to voice mail. She left a massage and also decided to text him. After he did not return either communication she decided to call Marcus.

"Hello?"

"Marcus this is Tiffany."

"Oh, hey, Tiffany, are you okay?"

"No, actually I'm not. The police just left here looking for Kiki. They think he was involved in a shooting that has a boy in the hospital. I don't know where Kiki is. I just don't feel like being alone.
Could you come over?"

"Sure I will come over. Let me get dressed and I will be there within thirty minutes."

"Okay bye." Tiffany said then hung up.

She felt stressed out. That is the time, when a good orgasm did her good. She did not think that she could wait on Marcus. She needed to experience an orgasm right then. She went over to her drawer and pulled it open. She dug under her socks, looking for her vibrator. It was not there. The DVD was missing also. She started going through all of her drawers. Still she did not find them. She realized that Cliff must have taken them. In a fit a rage she started throwing things across the room. She made so much noise, that she woke up the kids.

There was a soft knock on her bedroom door. She went and opened it and there stood Keisha crying.

"Are you alright, mommy?" she asked. Tiffany looked out into the hallway and saw that Donte and Angie were standing out there

"I'm alright baby, y'all go on back to bed, I'm okay." They all headed back to their bedrooms.

Tiffany was about to go back into her room, when she heard knocking at the front door. She went downstairs and opened the door.

Marcus walked in. Tiffany closed the door.

"Thank God!" she said as she started taking off her clothes. Marcus stood there, not understanding what she was doing. He had come over to comfort her after she told him what happened with Kiki. Evidently she had sex on her mind. He knew that he met her at a psychiatrist office, so she had to have some mental issues.

"Whoa, Tiffany I thought you were trying to find out what is up with Kiki?"

"I told you that you talk to damn much. I need to cum right now. That is the only way that I will be able to relax, so come on." she told him as she walked over to the couch and bent over it resting her arms on the back of it.

Marcus thought to himself, "Yeah, she got issues," he walked over behind her and undid his pants. He let them fall down to his ankles and did the same thing with his underwear. He took his dick and put it inside of her. Tiffany let out a sigh.

"Go slow," she told him. Marcus slow stroked her. Tiffany said "Yeah, that's it just like that." she closed her eyes and savored the moment.

"Okay, I'm ready now, fuck me Marcus."
New Flavor Books

Marcus picked up his pace. Tiffany wanted it faster but, she also wanted it harder.

"Bang me," she told him. Marcus started to pound her. They were both oblivious to the fact that Angie was sitting on the stairs watching them.

Angie had heard the knock at the door, and her mother going downstairs to answer it. After ten minutes and her mother not coming back upstairs, Angie decided to go and investigate.

She seen that her mother was having sex with a man that she had never seen before. Angie decided to sit down on the stairs and have a front row seat to watch the action.

Tiffany told Marcus, "I'm almost there, do it a little harder." Marcus put his hands on her shoulders and fucked her harder. Moments later Tiffany's body started to tremble. She started pushing her ass back to meet his thrust.

"Oh yes! Oh yes! Marcus ... Marcus!" she screamed out as she started to cum. Her pussy muscles began to constrict pulling Marcus' nut from him.

As soon as Marcus withdrew his dick from her, they started hearing clapping. They both looked towards the steps, "Good show ma." Angie said as she got up and started up the steps.

When she got to the top of the steps, she turned around and said, "Oh ma, by the way, I am pregnant." Tiffany did not even know how to respond.

"You see that shit? That's why I'm going crazy. These kids are going to be the death of me. Shit I'm stressed out all over again. Do you have a cigarette?"

"No, I do not smoke." Marcus told her as he was putting his clothes on.

Tiffany did not even attempt to put her clothes on. She just flopped down onto the couch naked.

"Listen, Tiffany, I do not know what all that you're going through, but it is evident that you are having very serious problems right now. I am going to tell you that I enjoy the sex with you very much. Tiffany, I also like you as a person and would like to get to know you as such. It is not all about sex with me, that is nothing. It is the connection to a person that matters to me. Now I am not going to pressure you, but I do want you to know that I am willing to make your problems my problems. With that being said, I have to go. You think about it."

He leaned over and gave her a kiss on her forehead, then got up and headed out of the door.

Tiffany just sat there and started crying. She just wanted to get away. She wanted to end all the pain and suffering. She got up and went upstairs. She went into the bathroom, opened up the medicine cabinet and started grabbing pill bottles out of it. There were seven bottles. She took them into her room, and opened them. She took two pills out of each bottle. She grabbed her bottle of Prozac and took two pills out of it. She made a sixteen pill cocktail. She started to dryly take them. After she took them all she laid down on her bed. Within thirty minutes, the cocktail started to take effect. She broke out sweating profusely. Her heart rate went up. Her body started to convulse and her arms went flailing. She ended up knocking over a lamp and it crashed to the floor.

Angie, who was still sitting up in her room heard the crash and decided to go and investigate. When she approached her mother's room, she saw that the door was wide open. When she got to the doorway, she saw her mother naked flopping around on the bed.

She ran over to her. "Ma! Ma! Get up!" Tiffany was foaming from the mouth. Angie ran to the phone and dialed 911. She told the dispatcher that her mother was having a seizure. The dispatcher instructed Angie to turn Tiffany onto her side, so that she wouldn't drown in her own saliva. Then she told her to stick a spoon or a hard object into Tiffany's mouth, to prevent her from swallowing her tongue. She told Angie that assistance was on the way.

The dispatcher stayed on the phone with Angie until the paramedics arrived.

Angie rushed downstairs to let them in. Three paramedics entered the house, and Angie led them upstairs to her mother's room. Tiffany was no longer moving. She laid still on the bed. One of the paramedics checked and seen that she had a weak pulse. Two paramedics loaded Tiffany onto the gurney. The third paramedic looked around the room and noticed all of the open pill bottles. He then knew that they were dealing with a possible suicide attempt.

They carried Tiffany downstairs, out of the house and put her into the ambulance. Once she was in the ambulance they put an oxygen mask over her face and began to pump her stomach.

Angie road with her mother in the ambulance to the hospital. Angie loved her mother no matter what. She did not want to see any harm come to her mother. She just wanted her mother to get herself together and to give her the love that she had been yearning to get from her for her entire life.

When they got to the hospital, the paramedics rushed Tiffany into the emergency room. While they were tending to her, Angie went to the phones. After several times of trying to reach Cliff, she decided to call her grandmother. Her grandmother answered the phone sounding as if she were asleep, "Hello?"

"Nana, this is Angie. They got my mother up here in the hospital."

"What hospital is she at?"

"Charity,"

"What is wrong with her, Angie?"

"They said that she took too many pills. She was unconscious. I did not know who else to call."

"I'm on my way up there, child. Where are your brothers and your sister at?"

"Donte and Keisha are at home. I don't know where Kiki is at."

"Alright, I do not have a car. I am going to have to call one of her brothers to come get me, I will be there." "Okay," Angie said then hung up.

Chapter 31

Tiffany's mother called her son Raymond. His wife answered the phone.

"Hello?"

"Lady, put Raymond on the phone."

"Okay, hold on," Lady shook Raymond who was asleep, "What?" he angrily said after being awakened from his sleep.

"Your mother wants you on the phone." He grabbed the phone, "Hello?"

"I need you to come take me up to the hospital."

"For what?"

"Your crazy ass sister done tried to kill herself."

"Why can't you call a cab?"

"Boy! If you don't get your big head self out of that bed and come get me, I know something. That is your damn sister, now get your ass over here!"

"Let me get dressed."

"Hurry up, Angie is up there by herself."

"Okay, I'm coming." he said then hung up.

While Raymond was getting dressed he thought, "Why did she have to call me. She could have called Robbie." Raymond and Tiffany had not been close since they were kids. The only time they saw each other was at the family reunions. He was surprised to hear that somebody had married her after she had four kids by four different men.

"What happened?" Lady asked.

"Tiffany's loony ass done tried to kill herself, too bad she ain't succeeded."

"Boy, that's your sister, don't talk like that."

"Yeah ... Yeah I'll be back." he said as he grabbed his keys off of the top of the TV. He got in his car and headed to his mother's house.

β

After they pumped her stomach they hooked Tiffany up to an IV. She had regained consciousness. She was Lucky, if Angie had not heard that lamp fall and decided to investigate, Tiffany would have surely died.

After stabilizing her, she was admitted into a room. They decided to keep her under observation for the next twenty four hours. They also wanted to have her talk to the hospital's psychiatrist.

Tiffany still felt weak. She laid on her bed in a dream state. Angie sat in the room with her. She pulled a chair up alongside of the bed. She watched her mother as she slept. She looked so peaceful. Tiffany's eyes blinked twice then she opened them. She looked over at Angie.

"Hey," she said.

Angie smiled, "I wasn't successful, huh?"

"I found you and called 911."

"You saved me? I thought that you hated me."

"I don't hate you, ma. I don't like some of the things that you do,   but   I   do   not   hate   you."

"I know I have been messing up my whole life. I done caused everybody so much pain, even myself. I thought that if I left this world that everybody's pain would go away including mines."

"You thought wrong, we love you and you are all that we have. Without you we would have been in more pain."

"Angie I am so sorry for the pain that I have caused all of you. I was trying to get myself together. I really was. I have just been feeling as if the walls are closing in on me and I need a way out." Tiffany and Angie both had tears in their eyes.

Tiffany's mother waltzes into the room, "Why all the tears? What are y'all crying for? And Tiffany what the hell is wrong with you trying to kill yourself? Got me out here this time of morning, you are lucky that your brother got his ass up out of bed to bring me up here."

"Angie, could you step outside so that I can talk to your grandmother right quick?"

"Okay," Angie left out of the room and decided to go and look for the vending machines to get herself a soda.

Tiffany's mother asked her, "So what is your problem child. It is always something with you."

"Ma, all you ever do is criticize me, you never support me."

"You ain't never did shit right for me to support you. You have been hot in the ass since you were a child. Chasing behind all them boys. Having all those kids with different people."

"There is a reason behind everything. I have been seeing a psychiatrist, trying to find out what is wrong with me. The doctor thinks that something may have happened to me when I was a child that traumatized me."

"Something like what?"

"She thinks that I was sexually abused, and that I have blocked the memory to keep from facing it."

"Tiffany, that's bullshit and you know it. You just love drama. So who do you think it was that did something to you?"

"I don't know, but lately I have been having this dream where I was a kid and this person was having sex with me. It happened more than once. I cannot see his face in the dream but his voice sounds familiar. I just can't place it."

"Child, you really are going crazy. That psych doctor that you are seeing needs to give you some medication to cure all that craziness in your head."

"Ma, you know what, I don't need this right now. Why don't you just go? You never cared about me anyway."

"If I didn't care about your ass, I would not have cussed your brother's ass out for not wanting to bring me up here. I just don't have time for this madness, Tiffany. You have always lived in this little fantasy world. It's hard for me to believe anything that comes from you."

"Well, my doctor is getting me to see a person that specializes in hypnosis. He says if they put me under hypnosis then they can dig deep into my subconscious to find out who the person in my dream is."

"Well when you find out who it is, you call me and let me know. I see that you are okay, so I am going home and going back to bed."

"Ma, which one of my brothers came with you up here?"

"Raymond, why?"

"Why didn't he come in with you?"

"Child, I don't know. He is probably in the car asleep. You call me when you find out something." Tiffany's mother told her on her way out of the room.

Chapter 32

Tiffany's mother got back in the car with Raymond.

"Wake up, let's go." Raymond woke up.

"So what happened? Why did she try to kill herself?"

"Boy, that girl done gone crazy. She was in there babbling about she think she got molested as a kid. She thinks that is why she has been doing all the crazy shit that she has been into all of her life."

"She ain't say who molested her?"

"She says that she has been having dreams about him, but cannot see his face in the dream. She said some quack doctor is supposed to hypnotize her, so that she can see the face." Raymond put a worried look on his face.

"Maybe I should go in there and talk to her."

"Boy, your ass is about to take me home. Ain't nobody got time for that girl's mess." Raymond pulled off. He figured that he needed to have a talk with Tiffany. He decided that he would come back to visit her the next day, and try to talk some sense into her.

β

The next day, Tiffany was sitting in her room waiting on the doctor, who needed to sign off on her release papers. She had been arguing with the nurses all morning. She had been telling them that, she needed to get home, because her kids were at home with no one watching over them. They told her that she was going to have to wait until she talked to the staff psychiatrist to be cleared. It was almost three o'clock and he had yet to arrive.

At 3:15pm she heard footsteps approaching her room. She thought that finally the doctor had arrived. She was surprised when the person that entered her room was not the doctor. It was her brother Raymond.

"What's up sis?"

"Nothing, waiting on the damn doctor, so that I can be released."

"I'm sorry that I did not come in last night, I was dead tired."

"That's okay,"

"So, are you good now?"

"Yeah, I'm alright."

"What's this momma talking about you seeing a shrink and is about to be hypnotized?"

"They think something may have happened to me as a kid and that I have a mental block or something."

"Tiffany ain't nothing wrong with you. You don't need a damn shrink. You pay them and they let you tell them what is wrong with you. You can do that with anybody."

"I haven't been having anybody. Me and Cliff are on rocky terms, the kids are upset with me and momma only downs me."

"What about me?"

"Yeah right, when was the last time that we talked?"

"That goes both ways Tiffany. You have a phone just like I have one."

The doctor finally walked into the room, "Sorry for the hold up. I was caught up with another patient."

"I'm ready to go."

"Okay, this won't take long. I just need to ask you a few questions. Then you can be on your way." He turned to Raymond, "If you will excuse us. I need to talk to Mrs. Smith alone."

"Okay, Tiffany I'm going to wait on you to give you a ride home.

I will be out in the hallway."

"Alright," Raymond left out of the room and the doctor began asking Tiffany questions.

"How are you feeling today?"

"I'm fine,"

"So, you do not have any more urges to harm yourself?"

"No I do not,"

"Are you sure?"

"Yes, what I did was a mistake. I will never do anything like that again."

"You do know that you are very lucky. If your daughter had not found you when she did, then we would not be here having this conversation. Mrs. Smith death is final. There is no coming back from it. So the next time that you feel low, find somebody to talk to. It says here that you have a private doctor that you are seeing. I suggest that you get their home number and pager number so that you will be able to contact them at anytime you need to. Now I am going to sign your release papers and you are free to go."

"Thank you, doctor."

A nurse brought Tiffany the clothes that Angie had brought to the hospital with them. She got dressed and left the room.

Raymond was waiting for her in the hallway. They walked outside to his car. Once they were in the car, heading towards Tiffany's house Raymond started back up.

"Like I was saying sis, you don't need to be seeing no psych and getting hypnotized. That shit might fuck you up. You think you got problems talk to your family or friends. All that stuff about you being molested is nonsense. You would remember something like that."

Tiffany was half listening to Raymond. He had never been concerned about her before, so she didn't know why he was being so concerned then. She just let him continue to talk. She nodded her head here and there acting as if she were paying attention to everything he was saying. When they pulled up in her driveway, he told her, "You don't need to see no shrink. Talk to me or mommy." Tiffany got out of the car and he pulled out of her driveway.

When she got in the house the kids were at the kitchen table eating. She knew that Angie must have cooked for them. When the kids seen her, their faces lit up. Keisha got up from the table, ran over and wrapped her arms around Tiffany, "Mommy! mommy!" she jumped up and down jubilantly.

"Are you hungry ma? I can fix you a plate." Angie asked her.

"No I'm tired, I'm going to lie down for a little while." she started to walk out of the kitchen, but turned back around.

"Has Kiki been here or called?" they all shook their heads no.

β

Cliff was over to Greg's house watching the Celtics and the Bulls game. There were about ten guys over there. Most of them were relatives. They were smoking and drinking, while watching the game.

By the third quarter most of them were buzzing.

Greg had been drinking straight shots of Gin and was totally drunk. Cliff had gotten drunk also. He became talkative. He just started talking out loud.

"Man, fuck these bitches. I'm about to get a divorce and go back to the old me."

Greg drunkenly replied, "You should have never married the slut bitch anyway, everybody fucking the hoe!"

"Fuck you mean everybody fucking her? Ain't nobody fucking my bitch."

"Nigga, you a fool, I been fucking that bitch since y'all got married. She done sucked my dick all up in your mother's bathroom at the cookout. Your little stepdaughter caught me fucking her in y'alls bed last week, when she came home from school early."

Cliff became enraged, "So your bitch ass played me like that?"

"Nigga, you played yourself, marrying that trick ass bitch. I done heard that the Arabs at the store down the street from y'all done trained the bitch, and on the low I heard that nigga Mike fucked her on your wedding day."

"Man, shut your lying ass up, before I fuck you up!" Cliff said as he approached Greg.

"Y'all chill man, y'all are family, fuck a bitch," one of the cousins said.

"Fuck that, this nigga say he fucked my bitch, in my bed, we ain't family. I'm about to see this nigga!" Cliff said as he lunged at Greg. People stood between them, not allowing them to get to each other.

"Let his bitch ass go. His bitch fucking everybody and his dumb ass is the only one that doesn't know about it."

Cliff struggled to get loose. Two of his cousins, forced him outside onto the porch. Once out there they begged him to chill.

"I'm good, let me go. I'm about to roll out." they let Cliff go and he went and got in his car and drove off.

The cousins re-entered the house. Neither considered locking the door. Everybody was in the living room questioning Greg about Tiffany.

"Were you really fucking that bitch?" his cousin Andy asked him.

"Hell yeah, that hoe is a cold freak. The bitch sucks balls, lick ass, the whole nine."

They were all laughing. No one noticed Cliff walk in through the door with a pistol in his hand. He entered the living room.

"What's up now, nigga?" Everybody turned in his direction, with shocked looks on their faces.

"Come on Cliff!" one of the cousins began before the shooting erupted. Greg being drunk was too slow to react. He got hit twice in the chest, once in the arm and once in his left hip. No one else was hit. Cliff calmly walked out of the house. He got into his car and drove off.

When Cliff left, his cousins carried Greg out to one of their cars, laid him across the back seat and headed for a hospital.

Cliff headed home to confront Tiffany. He ran every stop light and stop sign that he came to. When he got to the house, he drunkenly got out of the car and staggered up to the house. He opened the door, stepped in, pulled out his gun and headed upstairs. The house was quiet. He got to the bedroom and opened the door. Tiffany was lying on the bed asleep.

Cliff walked over to the bed, reached his arm out and put it around her neck. Tiffany's eyes flew open. Cliff had the gun pointed at her forehead.

"I should kill you bitch. You fucked my cousin and my best friend. I was that dumb, huh? Say something bitch!" Tiffany laid there terrified, with tears running down her cheeks.

Cliff grabbed her by her hair and pulled her from the bed. He slammed her to the floor.

"Stop Cliff! Stop!" Tiffany screamed.

"Bitch I done killed my family. I might as well kill you too."

Tiffany thought to herself, "I never thought that things would end this way. I was given a second chance to live, now I'm about to die."

Cliff pulled the trigger but nothing happened. He cocked the hammer back.

"Cliff!" he turned and there stood Angie in the doorway.

"You're just like your mother, huh? I should have fucked you the other day. I saw how you kept staring at my dick. I tried to do right by you. I covered for you, but all this time you have been covering for your mother." Angie just stood there crying. She knew that Cliff was referring to her catching Greg and Tiffany fucking.

"What's wrong?" Angie turned around and there stood Donte and Keisha. Tiffany was curled up in a fetal position on the floor.

Cliff took in all the kids standing there. Now Keisha was crying. He let go of Tiffany's hair and stood up. He headed out of the room. He told Donte, "Get your little faggot ass out of the way." as he walked out of the room. The kids rushed over to Tiffany and helped her up off of the floor and onto the bed.

"Do you want me to call the police?" Angie asked.

"No, don't do that, he just needs to cool off."

Cliff jumped in his car and took off driving recklessly. He ran the stop sign at the corner of their street. He heard sirens and looked into the review mirror. He saw that a police car with flashing lights was behind him. He stuck the gun under his seat, while pulling over.

The officer approached the car. Cliff rolled the window down and the stench of alcohol filled the officer's nostrils.

"Have you been drinking sir?" the officer asked Cliff.

"Just a couple of beers officer." Cliff said slurring.

"Could you please step out of the car? I would like to give you a field sobriety test." The officer reached for Cliff's door handle and opened the door. Cliff drunkenly climbed out of the car. He stumbled when he stood up. He put his arms out and leaned on the car for support.

The officer asked him to walk to the back of the car. Cliff kept one hand on the car as he walked and stumbled to the back. The officer radioed in for back up. He told Cliff to stand right there as he walked back to his patrol car. He reached inside of the car and pulled out a field sobriety test kit.

He walked back over to Cliff and put the device together. He had Cliff blow into it and the machine registered 1.8 which is over the legal limit.

"Sir, could you please walk back to my car." Cliff walked to the back of the police car where the officer opened the back door and loaded him into the back seat. The officer walked back to Cliff's car and opened the driver's side door. He bent over inside of the car and started searching it. He checked the sun visor, inside of the ashtray and the glove compartment. He dug in between the seats, and then checked under the seats. From under the driver's seat he pulled out a .38 Smith and Wesson. He noticed that the gun felt warm. He put it up to his nose and could smell gun powder, which indicated that it had been recently fired. Back up finally arrived, it was a sergeant.

"What do you have?"

"This guy ran a stop sign, I initiated a traffic stop. When he rolled the window down the car reeked of alcohol. I had him step out of the car and gave him a sobriety test. He registered 1.8 at which time I placed him into the back of my patrol car. Then I went and conducted an incident to arrest search and found this firearm under the front driver's seat." The officer held up the gun, which was now in a plastic bag.

"Did you read him his rights?"

"No, since I was by myself and he was clearly drunk, to prevent anything from going wrong, I just put him in the back of the car. He is not even cuffed."

"Okay let's affect the arrest." They had Cliff step out of the car, and then put handcuffs on him then read him his rights.

The officer called for a tow truck to come to the scene. Once the truck arrived, the officer pulled off, taking Cliff to the precinct.

Chapter 33

Kiki parked his car two streets over from his house. He crept through backyards and climbed over fences, until he reached his own backyard. He entered the house through the back door, which led into the kitchen. It was two in the morning, so he thought that everyone would be sleep. He intended to creep into the house and grab some clothes and dip back out. He did not know if the police were watching the house or not, but he did not want to take a chance. He waited until late at night to go home. He also did not want to hear his mother's mouth. He figured that if he crept in while everyone was asleep, that he could not bump heads with her.

When he entered the kitchen, he headed straight to the refrigerator to get something to eat. He had not eaten a good meal in the last couple of days.

He grabbed some turkey and mayonnaise, then went to the cabinet and grabbed a plate and a loaf of bread.

Tiffany and the kids were still huddled up in her room. They heard noise downstairs and assumed that Cliff had come back. For the safety of the kids, Tiffany thought it would be best to call the police. The 911 dispatcher advised Tiffany to lock herself and the kids inside of her room until the police got there.

Kiki finished his sandwich, downed a glass of orange juice and headed upstairs. Tiffany and the kids heard the footsteps coming up the stairs. They instantly thought that Cliff was coming to finish what he had started, they stayed quiet. Instead of the sounds of the footsteps coming their way, they went into the opposite direction.

The footsteps went towards the other end of the hall.

"What do you think he is doing?" Angie whispered.

"I don't know." Tiffany said.

Donte said, "I'm going to see what he is doing."

"Boy, are you crazy. You stay right here!" Tiffany told him. Even though Donte was gay, every since he came out he had a new sense of confidence about his self. Gay or not, he felt that he was still a man, and as a man he had to protect his family. He walked over to the door and opened it, "Donte! Donte get back in here!" Tiffany said in a low voice. Donte closed the door behind him as he left out of the room.

Kiki was in his room, snatching clothes out of his drawers and stuffing them into a pillow case.

Donte heard the shuffling of the drawers and headed in the direction that the noise was coming from. He stopped at his bedroom and grabbed a large pair of scissors. He proceeded down the hall. He stopped in front of Kiki's room. That is where the noise was coming from. He put his ear to the door and listened. He heard footsteps approaching the door. He backed away from the door and raised the scissors up, getting ready for a confrontation.

The bedroom door opened and Donte lunged forward with the scissors. Luckily for Kiki, he held the pillow case in front of him. Donte did not wait to see who it was. He slashed forward with the scissors, and they embedded into the pillowcase. The force of the strike caused Kiki to drop the pillow case.

Donte seen that it was Kiki that he almost stabbed and put his hand up to his mouth with a shocked look on his face.

"What the fuck is wrong with you?" Kiki yelled at him. Hearing Kiki's voice, Tiffany and the kids ran out into the hall.

"What the hell is going on?" Kiki asked them.

"Cliff tried to hurt mommy." Keisha told him.

"I will kill that nigga!" Kiki said pulling out his gun.

"Boy put that damn thing up in front of these kids."

All of a sudden they heard banging on the downstairs door. Kiki headed towards the steps, with the gun at his side.

"No Kiki, that's the police. I called them thinking that you were Cliff. You have to hide. Give me that gun and go and hide in Keisha's room. Y'all go get in y'all's beds." Tiffany took the gun and went and hid it in her room. Then, she went down the stairs to answer the door.

"Who is it?"

"It's the police open up." Tiffany opened the door and was surprised at the amount of police officers that had responded. Four police cars were parked in front of her house facing each other. Several police officers knelt behind the cars, using them as shields, with rifles and firearms pointed towards her house. Two policemen stood on her porch. One of them asked her, "Is he still here, ma'am?"

"Uh, no he's gone."

"Would you like to tell us what happened?"

"We just had an argument and he left."

"In your call you reported that he had threatened you and your kids with a loaded firearm."

"I just said that so that the police would get here fast."

"Ma'am placing false 911 calls and giving false reports are felonies."

"I'm sorry officer, I was just scared and did not know what to do. He was drunk and I thought that he was going to get violent, so I called y'all, but before you got here he left."

"So there was no gun?"

"No sir,"

"And he did not harm you or your kids?"

"No sir,"

"Look behind me ma'am. That's a lot of officers that could be out preventing crime or responding to more serious calls. Instead they are here to protect you and your kids. Please do not make a call like that again. You get off this time with a warning."

"Thank you officer, it will never happen again." The officers got back in their cars and left.

Tiffany went back into the house. She went upstairs to Keisha's room. She opened the door.

"The coast is clear."

Kiki stepped out of the closet. The other kids came into the room.

They all huddled around Kiki. They knew that he was in trouble.

"Why did you do it Kiante?" Tiffany asked him.

"I wasn't going to just let them get away with what they did to me."

"But you did not think to sneak and do it or to hide your face. You must have wanted to go to jail."

"Ain't nobody see my face."

"Somebody saw something. The police came over here looking for you. They got an armed and dangerous bulletin out on you. They told me that if you don't turn yourself in, that you might get hurt. Now I'm not going to tell you to turn yourself in, but I don't want you out in the streets, where you could end up in a confrontation with them. They do not play fair."

"I got this girl that I am staying with."

"Who is she?"

"Her name is Mona. I have been messing with her for awhile. She is twenty and got her own house."

"And you are sure that you can trust her?"

"Yeah, I'm sure."

"Where is your car at?"

"I got it parked a couple of streets over."

"Kiki, you cannot be driving that car. The police are looking for it. Paint it, sell it, do something with it, but do not drive it. I want this girl Mona's number, so that I can check on you."

"Okay, but what happened with you and Cliff. Did he put his hands on you?"

"You don't worry about Cliff. You are in enough trouble as it is. I am not worried about Cliff. I am worried about you. I think I'm getting a divorce. It's time that I put my energy into my kids. I know that I have done a lot to hurt y'all, but I swear to y'all that I am going to get myself together. My doctor said that I am close to solving the equation. So please bear with me. I love y'all." Tiffany reached her arms out and everybody closed in around her for a group hug. They all shed tears.

Kiki broke the embrace and told them that he had to go. He assured them that he would stay in touch.

Chapter 34

Everybody from Greg's family was up at the hospital, even Cliff's mother, who was Greg's mother's sister. They were all waiting to get word on Greg.

He had flat lined twice. Each time they used electric shock to restart his heart. They had to clamp an artery and give him several pints of blood. He was still in surgery. The doctors told the family that there was a 50/50 chance of him pulling through.

Greg's mother wanted to know how the shooting was allowed to happen, with everybody being there. Randy, one of the cousins, told Greg's mother how Greg had been taunting Cliff about having sex with his wife. He told her that they were trying to fight, but that they had broken them up and took Cliff outside. Once Cliff got outside he got into his car and drove off. He told her that nobody thought to lock the door. Cliff popped back up in the living room with a gun in his hand and began shooting. Greg's mother went into an emotional fit.

"That tramp ass bitch! I'm going to kick that hoe's ass! They are blood and they let that slut come between them!" Cliff's mother did not speak. She knew that her sister was just venting. She was misplacing the blame. Greg was dead wrong for betraying Cliff his mother thought to herself. She started feeling guilty thinking that maybe she could have prevented what happened from taking place.

She knew that if Cliff ever found out that she knew about Greg and Tiffany that he would never forgive her.

She wondered where Cliff was at. She had called his phone numerous times, but it kept going to voice mail. She decided that she would wait for Greg to come out of surgery to find out his condition before she headed home.

Chapter 35

Rick was placed in recovery, after having two surgeries performed on him.

He had to have a punctured lung repaired and reconstructive surgery on his face. His father was upset and wanted to get to the bottom of why his son was shot. He turned to his daughter for answers.

"What all did you tell the police, Renee?"

"I told them that it looked like my old boyfriend's car leaving."

"Why the hell would your old boyfriend shoot Rick?"

"Cause Rick and two of his friends jumped him."

"Jumped him for what, dammit?"

"Rick did not like how he was treating me."

"You mean you fed Rick some bullshit, about how he was treating you." Renee started crying. She did not mean for none of what happened to go down. She knew that she was wrong for telling her brother that Kiki had gotten her pregnant. She just told Rick that because she was mad at Kiki for how he had treated her and her girls.

"Your little hot ass done started some shit that got your brother up here fighting for his life. I want your phone and Ipod and you ain't going out on any weekends for two months." Renee turned to her mother for help. Her mother just put her head down. Renee, through a tantrum screamed, "I hate both of y'all!" as she stormed outside.

β

The next day Marcus called Tiffany. He asked her was she okay and she told him that he could come over if he wanted to. He came over and they sat on the couch and talked. She told him about the incident with Cliff and the trouble that Kiki was in. She even confided in him that she was seeing the psych because of a sexual addiction. She even went as far as to tell him that Cliff does not satisfy her.

Marcus sat there and listened intently, digesting all that she was telling him.

Most men would have run for the door after hearing all that Tiffany was saying. Marcus was steadfast, as if he was up for the challenge. He just wanted a clear understanding, of the things that were going on in her life.

"So the psychiatrist told you that something happened to you as a child, and that could be the reason for your addiction?"

"Yes, I am supposed to go under hypnosis, to dig deep into my mind, to see if I can uncover the mystery."

"So let me ask you this. Say you do get to the bottom of your problem and the doctor can help you get over it, what will be up with you and your husband?"

"Me and Cliff are a done deal. I do not think that the damage that I have caused to our relationship can be repaired. Even without my problem, Cliff doesn't satisfy me sexually and is selfish. When all is said and done, I'm filing for a divorce."

"Tiffany as I told you, I like you as a person. Nothing in life is perfect. Everyone has issues. It is evident that you are brave enough to confront yours and are trying to resolve them. I told you that I am willing to be a friend. I will support you through your hard times and we can just see where things lead down the road."

"Even after I have told you about some of the things that I have done, you would still consider being with me?"

"Tiffany the past is the past and it is obvious that you are trying to move forward. As long as you are truly seeking change, then I'm ready to move forward with you."

"You know it's not just me. I have kids too, and they have their own set of problems. Kiante is in a world of trouble, Angie told me that she is pregnant and I don't even know if I am capable of dealing with that right now."

"Tiffany you have to work through things slowly. You can't just snap your fingers and everything will become okay. It's not like me and you are getting married tomorrow. I am willing to walk side by side with you slowly as you tackle each obstacle in your life. Everybody needs someone in their corner. The person that is supposed to be in your corner evidently was not strong enough to play the part. I am! I'm going to be your corner man. So get ready champ, we got a hell of a fight coming up." Tiffany got teary eyed. She reached over to Marcus and gave him a hug.

"Do you want to stay with me?" Tiffany asked him.

"If I did that it would be hard for both of us to fight temptation. Right now is not the time. We are starting on a clean slate. Let's start from scratch and take it slow." Tiffany could not believe that he was turning down a chance to have sex with her. She thought that he was right. She did need to fight her urges to have sex. She needed to find the strength.

β

Tiffany was sitting on the couch, when the telephone rang. It was a collect call from Cliff, she accepted.

"Tiffany what's up?"

"Oh, they got you in jail?"

"Aren't you glad that I am in here, now you can really be the hoe that you are."

"Cliff, I do not have time for no mess right now. I am going to hang up if you keep tripping."

"How could you do me like that Tiff? My cousin and my best friend?"

"All I did was take care of you and your kids."

"Cliff, it ain't got anything to do with you. I got a serious problem. I have had this problem before I met you. I never meant to hurt or betray you. I have a compulsive behavior disorder. Sometimes I just cannot control my impulses. That is why I decided to see a doctor, to figure out how to solve my problem."

"You waited until you fucked my cousin and best friend, before you decided to seek help. I done shot my cousin, Tiffany. I don't know if he is dead or alive. When he told me that he was having sex with you and doing things with you that you have never done with me before, I lost it. I did not care anymore. Now look where I am at."

"I am truly sorry Cliff that you did what you did, because of me. I hope everything works out for you in the end."

"Fuck you mean you hope that everything works out for me? What you through fucking with me or something?"

"Cliff we are not compatible, and after what you did to me in front of my kids, I could never trust you again."

"Ain't this a bitch? You fuck my family and best friend. I am the one in jail, because of your ass, but you say that you can't trust me?"

"Not as far as you controlling your violence no. I have decided that I am filing for a divorce."

"A divorce, this shit is unbelievable. Tiff I swear to God, I'm going to kill your ass. You dead, bitch."

"Bye Cliff!" Tiffany said then hung up the phone.

Chapter 36

Cliff was pissed that Tiffany had hung up on him. He could not believe how she was trying to play him, after all that he had done for her. He dialed her number back two times. The first time, she refused the call. The second time, she did not even answer the phone. He stood staring at the phone, feeling like a complete fool. She had crossed him. He was sitting in jail because of her, and she was filing for a divorce.

"Man, how dumb could I be?" he said to himself. He was so mad when he called Tiffany that he never got a chance to get to why he had really called her. He had called her, because he was trying to make bond.

So far he had not been charged with shooting Greg. He was only charged with a DUI and possession of a firearm. His bond was $2,500. That was only $250 through a bondman. His mother had a collect call block on her phone. The only other option he had was to call Maria. He dialed her number, she answered and he was surprised when she accepted it.

"Are you in jail?"

"Yeah, they got me down in the city."

"What did you do?"

"They got me for a DUI and possession of a firearm."

"So now that you are in trouble, you call me? It was fuck me the other day, Poppi."

"Listen Maria, I am sorry about the other night. I was drunk and upset. Can we please talk about that after I get out of here? Right now I need you to three-way me to my mother, so that she can bond me out."

"I do it for you, Poppi, me not an evil person, give me the number." Cliff gave her his mother's number. She clicked over and dialed it. When his mother answered the phone Maria clicked back over.

"Ma?"

"Boy, where the hell are you at?"

"I'm down in the city. I need you to give $250 to a bondman, to get me out before they put more charges on me."

"What the hell they got you in there for?"

"A DUI and possession of a firearm."

"All right, let me run to the bank to get the money then I will be down there."

"Ma?"

"What, boy?"

"Did Greg make it?"

"Yeah he pulled through, your dumb ass lucky. If he had died the police would have investigated until they got to the bottom of it."

"What do you mean?"

"Your cousins told them that it was a drive by shooting, and that they did not get to see the shooter's face."

"He is living so that is the end of it."

"Okay, I am going to be waiting on you to get here."

"Sit tight, your tail will be out of there in a couple of hours, and don't think that you are going back over to that bitch house."

"I ain't thinking about her." Cliff wasn't going to tell his mother that Tiffany wanted a divorce. He wanted to give the impression that it was him that was cutting her off. His mother hung up.

He told Maria that he would stop by and talk to her when he got out. He hung up from her, then went and sat on his bunk waiting for his name to be called to get released.

Chapter 37

Kiki's money had started to run low. He decided to go out on the block to get his hustle on. He told his girl Mona that he would be back. He jumped into his car and hit the back streets up to Wendy's.

Kiki would sit on his car in Wendy's parking lot and serve fiends all day. It was Tuesday, which was also known as jump out day. On Tuesdays and Thursdays plain clothes detectives in tennis shoes would ride four deep in regular cars. They would jump out on the blocks that drug dealers were known to hang on. Most of the time the officers in the back seat were as fast as track stars. They usually had enough wind to chase a person ten blocks or more without breaking a sweat.

At about 4:15pm Kiki was coming out of Wendy's with a single with cheese and a chocolate shake. Just when he was approaching his car, a four door black Chevy flew into the parking lot. Kiki knew that it was the jump out boys. He dropped the burger and shake and took off running. Two black officers jumped out of the Chevy while it was still moving and gave chase. The officer driving the car jumped the curb. He was intending to cut Kiki off. Kiki turned right down a side street. He ran through some people's backyard.

The officers that were chasing him split up. The officer driving the car quickly drove around the block. As Kiki was cutting through the yard he slung the dope that he had. When he came out of the yard onto the next street, he saw the black Chevy speeding towards him.

He went to turn back into the yard and was hit hard.

He got tackled like a wide receiver in the NFL getting hit by a linebacker while cutting across the middle. The officer that tackled him knocked the wind out of him. The black Chevy had pulled up onto the sidewalk. The other officer that had been chasing him came walking from the other side of the street.

Kiki was cuffed and put in the back of the Chevy. They placed him in between the two officers that had chased him. He was driven back to the Wendy's parking lot.

"That's your car right there ain't it?" asked the officer sitting on his left.

"No that ain't my car."

"Funny how you were heading towards it when we came in the parking lot."

"It ain't mine."

"If it ain't yours then you don't mind if we search it."

"Check his pockets," the driver said. The officer patted Kiki's pockets. He forced his hand into his right pocket and pulled out a set of keys.

"Well … Well …Well, let's see if one of these is the key to the buried treasure."

The officer climbed out of the car, walked over to Kiki's car, stuck a key into the driver's side door and turned it. The lock popped.

"Well, what do you know?" said the officer as he opened the door. Two other officers got out of the Chevy and helped him search the car. They dug into his seats, cut up the lining of his car

152

and took off his door panels. They did not find anything. One of the officers said he didn't take off running for nothing."

"Maybe he threw it." another officer said. He called to the officer that was still in the Chevy and told him to call in his plates. After five minutes, dispatch notified them that Kiki was wanted for questioning in a shooting.

He was only seventeen, so they took him to Juvie Hall, where he was processed.

Chapter 38

Greg's mother was at her house talking to three of her nieces.

"I want y'all to beat that bitch's ass. My boy is lying up in the hospital fighting for his life because of that bitch."

"So, what do you want us to do auntie?" Tiara asked her.

"I want y'all to go knock on that bitch door, and when she open it commence to whipping her ass."

"Where does she live?"

"Don't worry I'm going to take y'all over there myself. I want to witness that hoe getting her ass kicked firsthand, come on y'all." she told her nieces. They all climbed into Greg's mother's car and headed to Tiffany's.

β

Tiffany was sitting in the house watching TV. She had already cooked dinner and was just waiting on the kids to get in from school to make their plates. Actually she was nervous, because she had gotten a call from Dr. Sullivan's receptionist telling her that she had an appointment in two days with a Dr. Harris, who was going to perform the hypnosis. Tiffany did not know what to truly expect. She may find out something that could change her life forever. She hoped that it would change for the better.

There was a knock at her door, "Who is it?"

"It's Jennifer, is Tiffany here?"

Tiffany did not know a Jennifer, but she still opened the door. The other girls were standing on opposite sides of the door so Tiffany could only see one girl when she opened the door.

"Yes, may I help ..." that is as far as Tiffany got before the girl reached out and grabbed her hair. The girl started beating Tiffany on the top of her head. The other two girls jumped in and started hitting Tiffany.

Greg's mother got out of the car, "Bring the bitch down here!" All three of the girls started pulling Tiffany, and she lost her footing. She fell down and they drug her down the steps. Her body made a thumping noise upon hitting each step.

Angie, Donte and Keisha had just gotten off of their school bus. They were walking down the street towards their house, when they noticed three girls jumping on someone. They heard an old lady scream, "Beat that bitch ass!"

"That's mommy!" Donte said as he took off running. Angie and Keisha followed behind him.

Soon as Donte reached them, he started raining blows.

"Get off my mother bitch!"

He snatched one of the girls off of Tiffany and started beating her. The other two girls stood up as Angie and Keisha reached them.

Angie rushed one of the girls taking her to the ground. Keisha, who was only twelve, was no match for the other girl. The girl threw Keisha to the ground, and then turned and started kicking Angie. She kicked Angie twice in the stomach.

Angie quickly let go of her sister, cried out in pain and curled up into a fetal position.

Greg's mother went into her trunk and grabbed a crow bar. She cracked Donte in the back.

"Get up off of her, motherfucker!" Donte felt a tremendous pain shoot through his back. Tiffany had gotten up off of the ground and grabbed a brick out of her yard. She ran towards Greg's mother. When Greg's mother saw Tiffany running towards her with a brick in her hand, she ran back towards her car yelling at her nieces.

"Come on y'all! Let's go!" They all jumped in the car and sped off. Tiffany ran over to Angie, who was still lying on the ground curled up in a fetal position. She was clutching her stomach.

"What's wrong?" Tiffany asked her.

"My baby!" she cried. Tiffany ran into the house and called 911. Then she grabbed a pillow off of the couch and ran back outside. She put the pillow under Angie's head. She noticed that there was a pool of blood on the front of her pants. She knew that Angie was probably having a miscarriage. She started crying, "It's going to be okay, baby."

Donte was lying on the porch. He could not stand up straight. Every time that he would try a sharp pain would go through his back.

The ambulance came and transported them to the hospital. Everyone had to be treated except for Keisha.

They learned that Angie indeed had miscarried. The kicks to her stomach cause her to lose her baby. The blow from the crowbar cracked Donte's rib cage. He had to be fitted with a body brace. Tiffany only had to be treated for minor cuts and bruises. The hospital decided to keep Angie for 48 hours to make sure that she did not start back bleeding inside.

Tiffany decided to call Marcus for a ride home. He came and picked them up. He could not believe that a group of girls had actually come to her house and attacked her. He asked her, "Do you know who those girls were?"

"No, but I do know that Cliff's aunt was with them."

"Do you want me to take you to the police station?"

"For what?"

"What do you mean for what, Tiffany? They violated you. Came to your home and attacked you. Most of all is what they did to Angie. That's close to murder. You have to file a complaint."

"I guess you are right."

"I know that I am right" Marcus said as he headed down to the police station.

He took Tiffany to the precinct where she filed a report of what happened and filed a formal complaint against Greg's mother. After they left the precinct, Marcus convinced Tiffany to stay at his house. He told her that he had a spare room that the kids could sleep in.

When they got there, Marcus cooked for them. They ate, and then he showed the kids to the room that they were to sleep in. The room had twin beds and a 32" color TV.

Marcus asked Tiffany how she felt. She said that she felt drained.

"Would you like a bath?" he asked her.

"I do not have a change of clothes."

"Don't worry I have something that you can put on."

"I could soak in there for a minute."

"I will run you some bathwater."

Marcus went into the bathroom and ran water into the tub. He went into the cabinet under the sink and took out some rubbing alcohol and some cherry scented body wash. He poured some of the rubbing alcohol into the tub, and then put in some body wash. He pulled a towel and wash cloth off of the shelf for her. He stepped out and told her it's all yours.

Tiffany stepped into the bathroom and closed the door. She stripped out of her clothes and got into the tub. The water was hot and soothing.

Tiffany laid back until only her neck and face was out of the water. She laid in that position for ten minutes letting the water relax her. When the water cooled down she washed up and rinsed herself off. She stepped out of the tub and dried herself off. She wrapped herself in a towel, left out of the bathroom and headed into Marcus' room.

"I'm going to do something for you that will help you relax." Marcus told her.

He told her to lie on the bed on her stomach. He sat on the bed next to her. He had a bottle of body lotion in his hand. He squirted some of the lotion into his hand then sat the bottle down. He rubbed his hands together and started to gently massage Tiffany's shoulders. As he massaged the lotion into them, Tiffany felt a soothing effect. Tension started to leave her body.

Marcus worked his way down to her back, using his knuckles to knead into her back. Tiffany let out a soft moan, from the feeling of pleasure that she was getting from the massage. He squirted more lotion into his hands and proceeded to massage her thighs, calves and even her feet. Tiffany had never been pampered like that before. She felt so relaxed, that she almost fell asleep. Marcus removed the towel from Tiffany and started massaging her ass cheeks. He worked his way between her legs. He pushed her legs apart. Using his thumbs, he gently rubbed the crevices between her pussy and inner thighs. Tiffany sighed and spread her legs further out. Marcus lowered his head, stuck out his tongue and licked Tiffany's pussy from the back. Her body shook, when his tongue ran over her clit.

Marcus stretched out, laid on his stomach, with his head between her legs. His forehead was in the crack of her ass, as he ate her pussy from the back.

Tiffany raised her ass up off of the bed, giving Marcus better access to her pussy. Marcus blew his hot breath on her clit. He licked and sucked on it until Tiffany's body spasmed. Her whole body shook, and then she laid still.

Marcus rolled over onto his back. Tiffany turned onto her side, facing him.

"Feel better?"

"Definitely,"

Tiffany reached her hand out. She pulled his dick out of his boxers and stroked it until it was fully erect. She went to lower her head, when Marcus stopped her.

"You don't have to do that. This is about you, not me."

"But I want to," she said as she lowered her head and took him into her mouth.

She gave Marcus some toe curling head. He sat up on his elbows and watched her make love to his dick with her mouth. When he started to cum, he put her hand around the base of his dick to help her milk it. She jacked his cum out of him, swallowing it all. Even after he was empty, she kept sucking until his dick became too sensitive and he couldn't take anymore.

He pushed her off of him and curled up on his side like a baby and went to sleep.

Chapter 39

Two detectives went to interview Kiki at Juvenile hall. Both of the detectives were black and middle aged. They tried the normal good cop, bad cop routine with Kiki.

Kiki refused to fall for it. They started out, "Kiante I'm detective Mitchell and that is detective Sims. I think you know why we are here, don't you?"

"No, I do not."

"Come on, we know the story. We know that Rick and his friends jumped you and you went and shot him to get even."

"I ain't shoot nobody. I don't even know the guys that jumped me."

"Kiante your car was seen leaving the scene."

"That is not true. I do not even know where the scene was, because I was not there. What day did this shooting supposedly happen anyway?"

"On Thursday the 28th, at around eleven o' clock."

"Well, it couldn't have been me. I was at home with my girlfriend at that time."

"And who is this girlfriend?"

"Her name is Ramona Richards."

"And do you have an address and number where we can reach her at?"

"Yeah, her address is 2915 E.121st, and her number is 921-8345.

Talk to her she will tell you. It could not have been me."

"We will check with her and back with the witness, and then we will get back to you."

"Okay, y'all do that." Kiki said as he got up and left the interview.

The detectives left. When they got inside of their car Detective Mitchell turned to his partner, "You know if his alibi holds up, then we got nothing on him. The girl did not see the face of the shooter, and she only seen the back of a car that she thought could have been his. There is nothing concrete linking him to the shooting."

"Let's go check out his alibi and see if she falls apart." his partner told him.

They went to Ramona's house and questioned her. They tried every tactic that they could to trap her up and get her to change her story. She told them the same thing every time, that Kiki was at home with her on that day and time. They decided they would try Rick's sister again and see if she could provide them with something concrete. They needed her to be able to positively identify Kiki's car as the one involved in the shooting or they were going to have to let him go.

β

Cliff's mother waited on him to be released from the city jail. When he was released she met him in the lobby. They were walking out of the building, with Cliff in the front. His mother reached up and smacked him in the back of his head.

"Shit! What you do that for?"

"To try and knock some sense into your dumb ass. How the hell you shoot your flesh and blood over that bitch?"

"Ma, don't hit me with that bullshit. Just last week, you were the one telling me that she was a good girl and for me to stand by her. I tried to tell you that something was up with her. That bitch was playing me all along. And if Greg was flesh and blood he wouldn't have played me like that."

"Well, you're going to sit your ass down. Rhonda is mad as hell at you right now. Stay away from them."

"I got to see that nigga, Mike. I want to see what he got to say."

"What are you going to do? Shoot him too? Let the shit go, Cliff. She ain't any good and she ain't worth it. Don't destroy your life over that bitch. Oh, and Rhonda took your cousins over there and had them beat the bitches ass." His mother told him as she broke out laughing. "Rhonda said that she had to take a crow bar to Tiffany's son. That woman is crazy."

"She beat Donte's little faggot ass, huh?"

"And the daughters. They had a free for all over there. That's why I want you to sit still. You are staying at my house until shit cools down." she told him as she headed to her house.

Chapter 40

The next day Marcus took Tiffany and the kids up to the hospital to visit Angie. Afterwards he dropped them off at home. Tiffany had not been in the house for a minute, when the phone rang. When she picked it up, she heard the automated operator. Thinking that it was Cliff, she hung up. Seconds later the phone rang again. This time she picked it up and listened for the name of the person that was calling.

When she heard Kiki's name, she accepted the call.

"You in jail?" she asked him.

"They got me in Juvie Hall."

"How long have you been in there?"

"Since the night before last. I been calling, but nobody has been answering."

"We haven't been here."

"I shouldn't be in here too much longer. The detectives came to see me. They ain't got anything on me. They are going to check my alibi. My girl got me. She is going to tell them that I was with her the night of the shooting."

"I thought they had a witness against you?"

"They say that somebody said that they seen a car that looks like mine. They ain't see my face, they ain't get a plate number, and they can't prove shit."

"I got to go to the doctor in the morning. After I leave there, I'm coming to see you. Do you need me to bring you anything?"

"No, I'm good, I can tough it out for a few days."

"Alright I will see you tomorrow." Tiffany told him then hung up.

The next morning Tiffany got up bright and early. Her nerves were so shook, that against Dr. Sullivan's orders, she popped two Prozac pills. She made herself a strong cup of black coffee.

She sat downstairs waiting on Marcus. He was taking her to her appointment. He wanted to be there to give her support. She was to jittery to sit still, so she decided to go back upstairs and check on Donte. He was on bed rest due to his injury. Just when she had finished checking on him, there was a knock at the door, it was Marcus, "Are you ready?"

"Just let me grab my purse."

Marcus headed for Dr. Sullivan's office in order for Tiffany to be in a comfortable environment, they decided to conduct the hypnosis at Dr. Sullivan's office.

They arrived and the receptionist told them to have a seat. Moments later Dr. Sullivan stepped out of her office and called for Tiffany to step into her office. Marcus remained seated in the waiting area.

In the black leather chair sat a middle aged black man with salt and pepper hair. He stood up when Tiffany came in and Dr. Sullivan made the introductions.

"Tiffany this is Dr. Harris."

"Hello Tiffany,"

"Hello,"

"Are you ready for the procedure?"

"I guess so,"

"Dr. Sullivan gave me a briefing about your issue, and we are going to get to the bottom of it. I am going to have you lay down on the sofa. I am going to have you practice some relaxation techniques, and then we will begin the hypnosis." Tiffany laid down on the couch on her back. She had her feet up, with her arms folded across her chest. Dr. Harris instructed her to close her eyes.

"Now Tiffany I want you to take ten deep breaths. After you take each breath I want you wait ten seconds before exhaling." Tiffany took a deep breath, counted to ten in her head, then exhaled. She repeated the steps nine more times.

"Do you feel relaxed?"

"Yes,"

"Now I want you to think back to your childhood. Picture yourself at eleven years old. Can you see yourself?"

"Yes,"

"I want you to picture yourself with the faceless man from your dreams, having sex with you. Can you see yourself and the faceless man having sex?"

"Yes he is on top of me, my body is on fire."

"Can you see his face?"

"No, but I know him. We are in my room and he is talking to me."

"What is he saying, Tiffany?"

"He is telling me not to worry, that no one is going to know."

"Tiffany, I need you to go further back. See yourself at the age of ten. See yourself with the faceless man. Can you see yourself?"

"No,"

"You have to concentrate Tiffany. You are ten and the faceless man is having sex with you."

"It hurts, stop please stop."

"Who is it Tiffany? Look at his face. Who is doing that to you?"

"Stop Raymond it hurts."

"I promise I won't tell anybody, I promise."

"Tiffany who is Raymond? Who is he?"

"I'm your sister, we shouldn't be doing this. We are going to get in trouble." Tiffany starts crying.

"That's it, bring her out." Dr. Sullivan told Dr. Harris.

Dr. Harris brought Tiffany out from under the hypnosis. It did not make Tiffany forget what she had seen. The hypnosis broke through the barrier that she had put up in her mind to block out what had happened to her as a kid.

Even though she was now out from under the hypnosis, she was still crying as she saw visions of her older brother Raymond having sex with her.

Now it all made sense to her, why Raymond had come to the hospital to visit her. He was trying to keep her from going through with the hypnosis, so that she would not find out the truth.

"So Tiffany I can tell you that what we have uncovered has a 99% chance of being true. Now that we know what happened, Dr. Sullivan has a better understanding as to your sexual dysfunction and how it should be treated. So, how do you feel at this moment?"

"Like a great weight has been lifted off of my shoulders."

"Now you have some tough decisions to make. You have to decide how you want to proceed with the information that you have uncovered. What happened to you was illegal and immoral. You may be able to pursue legal action against the person. You would have to find out the statutes of limitation before you do that. Also you may want to confront the person, which could turn out to be very painful.

So, you have to think about those things. Do you think that you are up for the challenge?"

"Yes I am,"

"This person Raymond, do you still have contact with him?"

"Yes, he came to visit me last week, when he found out what I was about to do. He tried to convince me not to go through with it."

"He must have known that you would uncover the truth. If you confront him, he may try to deny it. He may not want to face the reality of what he did. I do not know if he continued to engage in that type of behavior after you, but it is apparent that at some point he did suffer from a psychosexual dysfunction. He may need a clinical evaluation. Now that my job is done here I will leave you in the care of Dr. Sullivan." Dr. Harris gathered all of his belongings he shook hands with Dr. Sullivan and left the office.

"Tiffany I am going to set another appointment for our usual date and time next week. At that time we will discuss treatment options."

"Thank you, Dr Sullivan, but I do not think that that will be necessary. I think I know how to deal with this. If by chance my method does not work, I will contact you about setting up an appointment."

"That will be fine." Dr. Sullivan told Tiffany as she got up and led her to the door.

Chapter 41

Marcus saw Tiffany coming out of the office and rose to his feet.

"So how did it go?"

"I will talk to you in the car. I need you to take me somewhere right quick."

"Okay, let's go."

They exited the office building, and got into Marcus' car. Tiffany gave him directions and he pulled off.

"So what did you find out?"

"It was my brother."

"Your brother? No way!"

"It was him, and it is time for me to have a talk with him."

Marcus pulled up in front of a small single family home and shut the car off.

"Do you want me to come in with you?"

"No, I have to do this by myself." Tiffany exited the car and approached the house.

She rang the doorbell and Raymond's wife answered.

"Tiffany hey come on in, I'm glad to see you, are you okay?"

"Yeah, I'm okay, is Raymond home?"

"Yes he is, come on into the living room." Tiffany entered and took a seat. Raymond's wife called out to him. He came to the top of the steps and looked down. When he seen Tiffany sitting on the couch, he knew that he would be forced to face the past.

He went down the stairs with a fake smile plastered on his face. He turned to his wife, "Honey, could you let me talk to Tiffany alone for a moment?"

His wife looked at him with a worried look on her face, "Sure, honey, I'll be upstairs."

When Tiffany was sure that his wife was out of earshot, she spoke.

"Raymond how could you do that to me. I'm your sister Raymond."

He did not even try to deny it, finally feeling free. He had been carrying that burden and the feeling of guilt for a long time.

"We were kids Tiffany."

"I was a kid and you took my innocence from me. My relationship with my kids and husband has been affected by what you done to me."

"Don't put all the blame on me. As I recall there were times that you truly enjoyed it. Sometime you even begged for it. So if anyone is to blame then we both are."

"How dare you try to turn this around on me? I was a child and you took advantage of me. What about your kids, Raymond. Have you been touching your daughters the way that you touched me?" Tiffany asked him while raising her voice.

"Are you crazy? I would never harm my kids."

"But, it was okay for you to harm me?" she said almost yelling.

"Tiffany, please keep your voice down in my house. Listen, I am sorry about what happened when we were kids. I cannot change the past. Now that it has come out, hopefully you can move on with your life."

"Yeah, I hope I can." Tiffany said as she got up and prepared to leave.

Raymond escorted her to the door. Before he closed it he called out to her one last time.

"I am truly sorry Tiffany!" When Raymond shut the door and turned around, he was surprised to see his wife standing at the top of the stairs.

"Did you touch my babies?"

"What the hell are you talking about?"

"I heard everything, I can't believe that you did those things to your sister. You are a monster. I am going to have my babies checked out, to make sure that your perverted ass has not violated them."

"Lady, you are talking crazy right now. It did not happen the way that she is trying to imply that it did."

"I am telling you Raymond, I am going to kill you if I find out that you have touched my babies in any type of way."

"I ain't got time for this shit!" Raymond said as he headed out of the house. He slammed the door behind him got in his car and drove off.

Chapter 42

Tiffany got back into the car with Marcus and asked him to take her to see Kiki.

"So how did things go in there?"

"As about as good as I could have hoped for. Surprisingly, he did not even try to deny it. He tried to put the blame on me."

"He really tried to pull that stunt?"

"He sure did, he would not even take total responsibility for his actions. To him, at ten years old, I begged for it."

"It seems that your brother may have some serious psychological issues. He might need to see a doctor."

"He told me that I should leave the past in the past. I guess he would say that. His life is just fine. My life is the one that has been turned upside down."

"Tiffany, you may not want to hear this, but I have to tell you. You are blessed. You almost died, and you were given a second chance for a reason. You have been set free by the truth. You can start fresh. You can rebuild your life and your relationships with your kids. And if you allow me to, I will be right by your side to support you. If you need time and space to figure out what you and your husband are going to do, then I understand."

"I have already told you that me and Cliff are a done deal. I am filing for divorce as soon as I get time. Also I think it would be better if I moved."

"You can always come and stay with me."

"No, I need to show my kids that I have changed. I do not want to move too fast. It will give them the impression that I am still jumping from man to man. I do not want them to think that."

"I understand perfectly."

"I really like you Marcus and appreciate everything that you have done for me. I can see us having a future together. I just want to take it slow, so that I can dedicate most of my time to me and my kids."

"As I said I can perfectly understand where you are coming from. I will not rush you into anything. If you want to take it slow, then that is what we will do?"

"Thanks, Marcus." They pulled up in front of Juvenile Hall.

"Do you want me to come in with you?"

"No, I need to talk to Kiki alone also."

"Okay, I will be right here." Tiffany got out of the car and headed inside.

Chapter 43

Once inside she was led into the visiting room and sat at a table. A minute later, Kiki was brought in. He sat in a chair on the opposite side of the table from her.

"How are you doing in here?"

"It ain't that bad. I had time to clear my head."

"That is good Kiante. Do not destroy your life based off of my mistakes. Just like there is a reason for your behavior, there is a reason for mine. Today I found out that I was molested by someone close to me as a child. It was not a onetime thing, it was ongoing. It traumatized me and affected the way that I acted and the way I saw things.

Now I won't go into the details about what happened to me right now, but know this I know where my problem with men and my sexual behavior originated from. I cannot change the past, but there can be a better future for us. I am asking you as your mother to give me a second chance. Let me start with a new slate. I have been doing a lot of thinking and I think I have figured out who your father is. I even went on the internet and located him. Also I gave his information to social services, to set up an appointment for DNA testing."

"What is his name?"

"His name is Jerry. When I contacted him and told him that you could possibly be his son, he was eager to find out."

"Now, I don't want you to get all excited then end up feeling down later. I am not 100% sure, so let's just take the test and see what happens, okay?"

"Yeah okay, so what is up with you and Cliff?"

"We are a done deal. I am filing for a divorce."

"So, are you messing with that dude Marcus now?"

"We are friends and that is it for now. I explained to him, that I have to repair the damage that I have caused to my children, before I can get serious with any man. He says that he understands that."

"I should be out of here in the next couple of days. The detectives have already went and talked to my girl. They ain't got anything on me. They are just trying to stall me out. Have me sit for a minute.

When I get out I need to get my car out of impound."

"We can do that, but most importantly I want you back in school. I want you to either go full time or enroll in GED classes. You have to get your education Kiante. Can you do that for me?"

"Yeah I can do that."

"Well let me get a hug so I can get out of here. I have to go up to the hospital and visit Angie."

"What is she doing in the hospital?"

"She was pregnant but she miscarried." After what Kiki had done to those guys who had jumped him, Tiffany was not going to tell him why Angie had miscarried.

"She should be home tomorrow." Tiffany told him.

"I'm not wishing bad on her, but she is too young to be having a baby anyway."

"Everyone makes mistakes. Right now she needs our support."

"Tell her that I said I love her and that I hope to see her soon."

New Flavor Books

"I will tell her." Tiffany got up to leave.

She left Juvie Hall and got back into the car With Marcus.

"I need to make one more stop if you don't mind."

"Where to?"

"Back up to the hospital to visit Angie." Marcus headed in that direction.

D M Gaines

Chapter 44

Lady waited on her kids to get out of school. She wanted to interrogate them to make sure that Raymond had not violated them. They had two daughters, Vivian who was fourteen and Nena who was eleven. When they came home from school, she told them that she needed to talk to them one by one.

First, she took Vivian into the room, "Vivian I am going to ask you a question and I want you to be totally honest with me. Do you understand?"

"Yes I understand, what is going on?"

"Are you having sex?"

"No, I am not having sex."

"So you are still a virgin?"

"Yes why?"

"So if I took you to see a gynecologist, it would be confirmed that you are still a virgin?"

"Yes mother gosh, what is going on?"

"Vivian at anytime in your life has anybody touched you inappropriately?"

"What do you mean by inappropriately?"

"Has anybody touched you or tried to touch you in a sexual manner?"

"No! Ain't nobody ever touched me like that."

"If someone ever tries to, don't be scared to tell me. Do you understand me?"

"Yes,"

"Okay, go and do your homework."

Lady then called Nena into the room and put her through the same line of questioning. She also said that she was never touched inappropriately.

Even after both girls, stated that they had never been touched sexually, Lady still did not feel comfortable.

At about 8:00pm Raymond returned home. When he entered the house he was surprised to see numerous garbage bags sitting by the door. Lady was sitting on the couch with her arms folded.

"What is all this?" Raymond asked Lady.

"It's your shit! I want you out of here, until you get help."

"What do you mean, until I get help?"

"It's obvious that you are sick. To do that to your own sister, and tell her that it was her fault, you need help."

"This is our house, Lady. I pay the mortgage. I am not going anywhere."

"Raymond, after what I have heard I cannot trust you around our daughters, until I know for sure that it's safe. If you refuse to leave I will call the police and tell them what I have found out."

"Lady, you are tripping. You did not tell that bullshit to our kids did you?"

"I asked them had they been touched, but your name didn't pop up."

"So what reason are you going to give them for me not being here?"

"I'm going to tell them that we are having problems and have decided to separate for a minute."

"And you expect them to believe that?"

"I don't care if they believe it or not. I want you out of here right now!" Raymond opened up the door and started carrying his bags out to the car. He put all of the bags into the trunk, got into his car and drove off.

Lady had made an appointment with the locksmith to have the locks changed the following day.

β

Raymond drove around fuming. He blamed Tiffany for fucking his life up.

"Almost twenty years later, she comes with this bullshit. Threatening everything that I worked for." he said to himself. He felt that if he lost his family, then he wouldn't have anything to live for.

"How could she do this to me?" he thought to his self. He headed across town saying to himself.

"That bitch is going to pay."

Chapter 45

Earlier, Tiffany arrived at the hospital to visit Angie. Once again Marcus was left in the car. She entered Angie's room. Angie was sitting up in bed. Her cheeks were stained with tears. Tiffany could tell that she had been crying. She approached the bed.

"How are you holding up?"

"I guess I am okay."

"Angie, I do not know where to begin. What happened to you was very tragic. Truly you are too young to be having a baby. You have your whole life ahead of you."

"It was for the best. I did not know who the father was anyway. Really I was just lashing out at you. Trying to go through what you went through, so that I would have a better understanding on why you are like you are."

"Angie the reason that I am the way I am is because I was molested as a kid repeatedly by someone that was close to me. Doing what you were doing would not have showed you close to why I am the way that I am. It would have just caused you to live a horrible life. What happened to me as a child affected my way of thinking and how I felt about myself. It may seem to you that I was having fun, but believe me I have been hurting inside for a long time Angie, and now I know why. So whatever you think of me, I want you to know that my behavior is not something that I am proud of and I would never want you to follow the route that I took. You have not been totally scarred. You can rebound and make something of your life, and I will be right there to give you the love and support that you need. Now, can I have a hug? Mommy needs one." Angie hugged Tiffany for about a minute, squeezing her tightly. They broke the embrace and Tiffany told her that she would be back to pick her up the next day.

Tiffany and Marcus left the hospital. Tiffany felt exhausted. She told Marcus to take her home. When she got in, she made dinner for the kids. She fed them, and then went upstairs to lie down. She did not even take a Prozac pill, but she instantly fell asleep.

Sometime during the night, she was awakened when she felt her breath being taken away from her. When she opened her eyes, a person with a mask on, was on top of her. He was choking her.

Tiffany wanted to scream, but the pressure around her neck prevented her from making a sound.

"You just couldn't leave well enough alone. You should have been dead bitch. You are dying tonight." The masked man said to Tiffany as he was choking the life out of her.

Tiffany was becoming light headed. She knew that she did not have much longer. She refused to just lay there and die.

She thought that she had too much to live for. She reached out with her hand and grabbed the masked man's scrotum. She dug her nails into his balls and twisted them. The masked man yelled out. Tiffany applied more pressure. The intruder let go of her neck. Tiffany quickly rose up and sunk her teeth into his chest. Her teeth sunk deep into his flesh.

"I'm going to kill you bitch!" he took his hands and pried Tiffany off of his chest. She came away with a chunk of his flesh in her mouth. He punched her in the face. Tiffany let go of his scrotum, reached her hands up and dug her nails into his face through the mask.

The masked man had thought it was going to be an easy kill. Now he was wishing that he had just brought a gun and shot her. He never would have thought that she had that much will to live.

Someone started banging on the door and yelling, "Mommy! Mommy open the door."

The masked man punched Tiffany in the face twice more, causing her to loosen her grip on his face. He then jumped up off of the bed and hurried over to the window. He climbed back out of the window the same way that he had entered through it. Tiffany quickly jumped off of the bed, ran over to the window, shut it and locked it then ran to her bedroom door and unlocked it.

Keisha and Donte were standing there. Donte stood half erect, with a pair of scissors in his hand.

"I called the police," he told Tiffany.

Tiffany helped him over to her bed, so that he could take the pressure off of his back and rib cage. Keisha was crying, "I'm scared, mommy." Tiffany knew that they were no longer safe in that house. She decided to call Marcus. She asked him if he could come and get her and the kids. He told her that he was on his way.

Tiffany and Keisha went around the house gathering up clothes and other things that they would need. There was a knock at the door. Tiffany and Keisha went downstairs. Tiffany opened the door. It was like dejavu. The same two officers that had responded the night that she had mistaken Kiki for Cliff were again on her porch.

"So Mrs. Smith, we are back again. Is it safe to say that something has actually happened this time?"

"Look at my eye, do it look like it belongs like that, or that something actually took place with it?"

"Okay would you like to tell us what happened?"

"I was asleep and woke up to a masked man choking the shit out of me. He was trying to kill me."

"And what makes you think that he was trying to kill you?"

"He said so while he was trying to do it."

"So he did not try to sexually assault you. His only intent was to kill you?"

"Yes,"

"And may I ask how you prevented that from happening?"

"I grabbed his balls and bit him in the chest."

"Ouch, you bit him in the chest?"

"Yes, I pulled a plug out of him. Also I dug my nails into his face through the mask. So there should definitely be marks on his face."

"And who do you think the person was?"

"My husband of course, he must have gotten out of jail. He called me a couple of days ago, telling me that he was about to get out and that he was going to kill me."

"Do you think you may know where he could be hiding?"

"Probably his mother's house."

"Do you have that address?"

"Yes," Tiffany gave the officers Cliff's mother's address. They told her that she would have to go downtown in the morning to file a formal complaint and to get a restraining order. Tiffany was escorting them to the door. She opened the door and Marcus was standing there. The officers immediately went for their weapons, "That's not him!" Tiffany yelled.

The officers relaxed and told Tiffany not to forget to go downtown in the morning and they left.

β

Marcus entered the house, "Look at your eye, are you ready to get out of here?"

"I have to help Donte down the stairs."

"Come on, I will help you."

Marcus and Tiffany went upstairs to get Donte. Marcus found that he could handle him by himself, so Tiffany and Keisha grabbed the bags of items that they had packed up.

They all got into the car and headed to Marcus' house.

Chapter 46

Raymond drove around in pain. He did not know where to go. He felt that he needed to get his chest treated. Tiffany had bitten a plug out of him.

His face was also stinging from the wounds left by her nails being dug deep into his face.

"I should have just gotten a gun and shot her ass. She is like an omen to me."

He decided to go to his mother's house, so that he could treat his wounds.

He arrived at his mother's house and rang the doorbell. Because his mother was a hard sleeper, it took her about five minutes to answer the door.

"Oh my God, what happened to you?"

"I got robbed."

"What are you doing out this late at night. Why aren't you at home with Lady and the kids?"

"We had a falling out. She wants time apart for a minute."

"What kind of nonsense is that, Raymond?"

"Ma, I really don't want to talk about it right now." he told her as he headed upstairs to the bathroom.

He went into the bathroom and opened up the medicine cabinet. He pulled out a bottle of peroxide and some band aids. He got some tissue paper, poured some of the peroxide on it and started dabbing the wounds on his face. He pulled his shirt off and examined his chest in the mirror. A chunk of flesh was missing from the middle. He thought that he might need some stitches.

His mother barged into the bathroom. He tried to put the shirt up in front of his chest, but he was not fast enough. His mother saw the wound.

"Boy, ain't nobody rob you. You got scratch marks on your face, and a plug bitten out of your chest. You sure that you and Lady wasn't fighting?"

"No ma, we weren't fighting. Let me finish what I am doing."

"You need to go to the hospital to get them wounds treated, so that they won't get infected."

"I will go in the morning. I am tired right now and want to go to sleep."

"The bed in the guest room is already made." Raymond finished putting on the bandages, and then went in to the guest room to lie down.

He fell into a deep depression, as he thought about the events that had transpired that day. He knew that he had to be thinking irrational to do the things that he did. He tried to kill his own sister. He realized that if he was going to do that then he should have done it before she let the secret out not afterwards.

He felt like his life was spiraling out of control. Lying there, he finally fell into a fitful sleep.

His mother could not sleep. She figured that it was more to the story then Raymond was telling. She quietly picked up the phone and called Lady. She answered on the fifth ring.

"Hello?"

"Lady, this is Tasha. Did you and Raymond have a fight tonight?"

"We had an argument earlier. That's about it."

"Did y'all get physical with each other?"

"No we did not, Ms. McCoy."

"Why are you and Raymond separating?"

"Ms. McCoy that is something that I would prefer that you talk to him about. I will say this though, I think your son needs some mental help."

"Why would you say that?"

"Again I think that you should talk to Raymond about it, then again you might want to talk to Tiffany about it."

"Tiffany, what do Tiffany's crazy ass got to do with anything?"

"Your daughter is not as crazy as you think. After what she has been through she is lucky that she ain't gone crazy."

"What are you trying to say Lady?"

"I have to go Ms. McCoy, talk to your son and daughter." Lady said then hung up.

Raymond's mother sat there on her bed confused. She wondered what the hell was going on. She picked up the phone and dialed Tiffany's number but got no answer. She tried two more times then gave up. She would try back in the morning.

Chapter 47

The police arrived at Cliff's mother's house at six o'clock in the morning. It was eight police officers altogether. They banged loudly on the door. Cliff's mother woke up, got up out of her bed and headed downstairs.

"Who the hell is banging on my door like that?"

"It is the police, open up." Cliff heard the banging too. He got up and made it to the top of the stairs by the time his mother was opening the door.

The police saw Cliff standing at the top of the stairs, "Ma'am we would like to speak to Clifford Smith."

"That's me, officers." Cliff said as he came down the steps.

"Could you please step outside, sir?"

"What is the problem?" Cliff's mother asked the officer.

"We need to take him down to the station for questioning."

"The first thing that came to Cliff's mother's mind was that it had something to do with Greg's shooting.

"What do y'all need to question him about?"

"We will explain it all at the station, ma'am. You can meet us there if you like."

"You damn right, I want to be there." she told the officer.

They placed Cliff in one of the squad cars and drove off. Cliff's mother called her sister. Rhonda answered, "What?"

"Rhonda, your ass done gave the police Cliff's name?"

"Hell no! What are you talking about?"

"The police just came and took Cliff. Talking about they wanted him for questioning."

"Well, it ain't got shit to do with Greg. Ain't nobody said that boy's name."

"Well, I'm about to go down there and see what the hell is going on."

"Do you want me to go with you?"

"That's alright, I will call you when I find out what is going on." "Okay," Rhonda said and they hung up.

Cliff's mother got dressed, grabbed her purse and car keys then headed out the door.

β

When the police got Cliff to the station, they took him into an interrogation room. Two detectives stepped inside of the room. They looked at Cliff as if they were examining him. Cliff just sat there and stared at the officers.

The two detectives stepped back out of the room. They stood outside of the door. One said to the other, "I don't see any marks on him."

"He doesn't look like he has been in any type of altercation."

"She said that she bit a plug out of his chest."

"Let me grab the camera right quick. The officer went and got a camera. They both stepped back inside the room.

"Mr. Smith could you please remove your shirt?"

Cliff stood up and pulled his shirt over his head. The officers looked at Cliff's chest then at each other. The officer with the camera stepped forward and started taking pictures of Cliff's face and chest.

"Could you turn around please?" He turned around and the officer took pictures of his back.

After that, they told Cliff that he could put his shirt back on and have a seat.

"So Clifford, where were you earlier tonight?"

"I have been in the house all day and night."

"At what house?"

"The house that y'all came and got me from."

"So, you never went to your wife's house tonight?"

"No man, we don't fuck around no more."

"For some reason she thinks that it was you that climbed through her bedroom window wearing a mask and tried to kill her."

"That's bullshit, I have been at my mother's house all night. She will vouch to that."

"We do not believe that it was you. She said that she left distinctive marks on the attacker, which you do not have. The pictures that we took of you are really for your benefit. We are still going to have to hold you while we clear this up. Just sit tight." The detectives left out of the room.

"Dan we have nothing on him. She did not see the attacker's face. This guy doesn't have any scratches or bite marks. Also he ain't walking like he almost had his balls twisted off. I say we wait until his mother arrives. If she confirms his story then we let him go."

"Sound like a plan. I don't feel like doing all that paperwork anyway."

β

When Cliff's mother got to the station, the detectives questioned her. After she confirmed Cliff's alibi, they released him.

Cliff and his mother were in her car heading home.

"They asked me where I was at all night but they wouldn't tell me why they needed to know."

"What happened?"

"Somebody with a mask on broke into Tiffany's house and tried to kill her."

"And they thought it was you?"

"I guess, but they said that she left marks on her attacker and I didn't have any, so I guess I'm good."

"They should have killed her ass. That bitch ain't nothing but trouble. You keep your ass away from that crazy bitch, I'm serious Cliff."

Cliff sat there wondering who the hell could it had been that tried to kill Tiffany.

Chapter 48

Eight in the morning Raymond's mother got up for work. She was still bothered by Lady's words about Raymond and Tiffany. She felt that she needed to know what was going on. She went into the guest room and woke Raymond up. He sat up in the bed.

"Raymond what the hell is Lady talking about that I need to talk to you and Tiffany?"

"Lady? When did you talk to Lady?"

"Last night while you were sleeping."

"What did she tell you?"

"She was just rambling, saying that you needed help and that Tiffany isn't crazy. I want to know what the hell is going on. I tried to call Tiffany, but she wouldn't answer her damn phone. Maybe I will stop over there when I get off of work."

"I'm going back to bed. I will talk to you when you get home from work."

"You better have some answers for me too." she told him as she headed out.

Raymond knew that if she went over to Tiffany's house and found out what happened last night that she was going to put two and two together. Then she would know that it was him that tried to kill Tiffany. Raymond only saw one way out. He went into his mother's room. He went into her closet and grabbed a shoe box off of the shelf.

Inside of the shoe box was a .38 revolver.

He took the gun out of the box and went back into the guest room. He grabbed a pen and a piece of paper and sat down and began to write. He wrote apologies to his mother, to Tiffany and to his wife and kids. In the letter he explained that he could not bear the shame that he had caused them and brought upon himself. He signed the letter and sat it on the night stand. He picked up the gun, put it to his temple and pulled the trigger.

Chapter 49

Marcus took Tiffany to view some houses that she had seen for rent in the paper. The third house that she viewed was a four bedroom single family home. Tiffany fell in love with it.

It had a finished attic and basement. Kiki could choose which one that he wanted to turn into his bedroom. Tiffany told the owner of the home, that she would like to take it.

The lady that owned the house asked Tiffany when she wanted to move in. Tiffany told her as soon as possible. They agreed that she would move in Friday.

Tiffany had Marcus take her to the house. She wanted to start packing some of their things.

Tiffany received two phone calls while they were at the house. First Kiki called and said that he was being released and needed a ride. She told him, that she and Marcus would be up there to get him.

She hung up the phone and told Marcus that Kiki was being released and that they needed to go and pick him up. They were getting ready to leave the house, when the phone rang again. Thinking that it was Kiki calling back, Tiffany rushed to the phone to answer it.

"Hello?"

"Tiffany where the hell have you been. I tried calling you all night." Tiffany was surprised to hear her mother's voice on the other end of the phone.

"I had to leave here last night. Someone broke in here and tried to kill me."

"Girl you never cease to amaze me. It is always something with you. If they tried to kill you, how did you get away?"

"I fought, I grabbed his balls, bit a plug out of his chest and dug my nails into his face."

"You bit him where?"

"In his chest," Tiffany's mother started putting two and two together. She was trying to figure things out in her head.

"Ma, I found out what happened to me as a kid. I think ..." Tiffany heard the phone click and realized that her and her mother had been disconnected. She waited a few minutes to see if her mother would call back. When she didn't, Tiffany and Marcus left to go pick up Kiki.

Tiffany's mother hung up from her and called the house. No one answered. She needed some answers, she told her supervisor that she needed to take the rest of the day off to deal with a family emergency.

She left work and went home. When she stepped into the house she called Raymond's name but got no answer. She went upstairs to the guest room. She opened the door and found Raymond sprawled out on the bed with her gun lying next to him.

She let out a deafening scream, and started to shake uncontrollably. She ran out of the room closing the door behind her and into her room to call 911. She stayed in her room until the police arrived.

She let them in and led them upstairs to the room. They saw Raymond lying on the bed dead, and notified the coroner and the CIU. The criminal investigation unit arrived on the scene. They dusted the gun for prints and checked Raymond's hand for traces of gun powder.

Re-Looking around the room, one of the investigators noticed a letter sitting on a night stand. He picked it up and read it. Then, he told Raymond's mother to take a look at it.

She could not believe what she was reading and collapsed to the floor. The officer radioed for the paramedics to come to the scene. They got there and found that her blood pressure was up. She was advised to take her medication and to lie down and relax.

Chapter 50

Tiffany and Marcus went and picked up Kiki. Then they went up to the hospital to pick up Angie. When they were all in the car, Tiffany told Kiki and Angie that they were staying at Marcus' house until they move into their new place on Friday.

"What about my car?" Kiki asked

"Kiki, I don't have no money to be getting no car out of the impound right now."

"I got it, do you know what lot it is in?"

"Yeah, it's in lot three." They headed to the impound. When they got there, Marcus paid the towing and storage fees.

Kiki hopped into his car and followed them to Marcus' house. They were all sitting at the kitchen table eating, when Marcus spoke.

"I would like to say something to your kids."

"I know that y'all do not know me very well. And I would never just jump into your business. I know that y'all have been through a lot. I just want to tell you kids that your mother is a very strong woman. I have come to know her dearly, and I know that she loves each and every one of you. She also values your opinions. I am trying to pursue a relationship with your mother, but she is concerned about how you will view her if she gave me that chance. So as a man, I am asking for your blessing to enter into a relationship with your mother." Tiffany sat there looking stunned. She could not believe that he had just done that.

The kids all looked at each other. Kiki spoke for them.

"Marcus you stuck by our mother through some crazy shit, some of which had to do with us. We know that you care for our mother, and as long as you make her happy, we do not have a problem with y'all being together." Marcus got up, walked over to Kiki and shook his hand.

Tiffany just sat on the couch crying. Tears were silently running down her cheeks.

"Why are you crying mommy?" Keisha asked her.

"Because I love y'all so much, and I'm just glad that I have y'all in my life." All the kids gathered around Tiffany and gave her a big hug.

β

Later that night Tiffany and Marcus were in the bedroom, when Tiffany decided to call her mother back, to see why they had disconnected. Her mother answered the phone crying.

"Ma, what is wrong?" Tiffany asked her. In between sobs her mother told her Raymond was dead.

Tiffany could not believe her ears. She thought that it just couldn't be real.

"How did he die, ma?"

Even after what he had done to her, he was still her brother and she still loved him.

"He committed suicide Tiffany. He left a note, saying that he could not deal with the shame of what he had done to you. I'm so sorry baby, I never knew. I swear I didn't. I truly apologize for the way that I have treated you. I have always loved you."

"I know that you didn't know ma, it's okay. I love you too."

"I have to make funeral arrangements."

"I will come over first thing in the morning to help."

"Okay baby, I'm tired, I'm going to go lay down."

Tiffany's mother went upstairs to lie down in her bed. She fell asleep, and never woke back up. She died in her sleep from a heart attack. The pain of what had happened to her son and daughter was too much for her weak heart to bear.

β

Tiffany found her dead the next morning when she went over there to help with Raymond's funeral arrangements. She and her brother Robbie made funeral arrangements for their mother and brother.

They had a double funeral and were buried side by side.

Raymond's wife and kids attended. Also Cliff's family attended.

Tiffany and Cliff did get a divorce and Tiffany never moved into the new house. Instead, she went ahead and moved in with Marcus.

Tiffany's relationships with her kids blossomed. Kiki got his GED, gave up selling dope and found a job. He moved in with his girl Mona, who was four months pregnant. Tiffany was just glad, that she was finally able to live a normal life.

New Flavor Books & Publishing LLC
Book Order form

Full Name: _____

Institution# (If applicable):_____

Address: _____

Address 2: _____

City:_____ State:_____ Zip:_____

Book Title:	Price/Quantity
Hood to Hood: A Cleveland Story	$14.99 ____
Hood to Hood 2: Spank's Revenge	$14.99 ____
Tiffany's Addiction: Director's cut	$14.99 ____
All Flavors A book of Erotic Short Stories	$9.99 ____
Deidre's Desires	$14.99 ____
Murder or Justice	$14.99 ____
Hittin' Licks	$14.99 ____
Gemini Killer	$14.99____

Total Including ($3.00) Shipping and Handling _____

To place an order for one of our books please send a payment for the price of the book plus $3.00 for shipping and handling to:

New Flavor Books & Publishing LLC

C/O Book orders

P.O. Box 603323

Cleveland, Ohio 44103

New Flavor Books
Please allow 2 - 4 weeks

www.ingramcontent.com/pod-product-compliance
Lightning Source LLC
Chambersburg PA
CBHW031336170626
46807CB00002B/729